Sarah. H̲ ̲ ̲ ̲ ̲ ̲ ̲ ̲ ̲ ̲ ̲ ̲r. A joyous re̲ ̲ ̲ ̲ ̲ ̲ ̲ ̲ ̲ ̲ate, aching need.

What was happening? How had this started?

But he knew how it had started. It had started six long years ago, when he'd first fallen in love.

In love.

The words slammed into some dark recess of his brain, registered, shocked.

She was his twin's fiancée. She was Grant's love. She had nothing to do with him. She was a part of him that had died along with Grant. A searing, aching pain that could never go away. An impossibility.

And she felt it. He could sense the moment when she tensed and moved back, just a fraction, so she could see his face. Her eyes resting on his were huge in the shadowed light cast by the table lamp. She looked ethereal. Not of this world.

She'd destroyed Grant, he thought desperately. She could well destroy him.

POLICE SURGEONS

Working side by side—and sometimes hand in hand—
dedicated medical professionals join forces
with the police service for the very best
in emotional excitement!

From domestic disturbance to emergency room drama,
working to prove innocence or guilt, and
finding passion and emotion along the way.

THE POLICE
DOCTOR'S SECRET

BY
MARION LENNOX

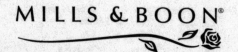

MILLS & BOON®

For Anne and Evan,
whose laughter fills my house and writes my books.

*First published in Great Britain 2004
Harlequin Mills & Boon Limited,
Eton House, 18-24 Paradise Road, Richmond, Surrey TW9 1SR*

© Marion Lennox 2004

ISBN 0 263 83931 1

Set in Times Roman 10¼ on 11¼ pt.
03-1104-54558

*Printed and bound in Spain
by Litografia Rosés, S.A., Barcelona*

CHAPTER ONE

FORENSIC pathologists weren't supposed to be cute.

Nor were they supposed to be Sarah.

Dr Alistair Benn stared at the crimson and white vision bouncing across the tarmac towards him and felt like leaving town. Now.

Leaving. Ha! As Dolphin Cove's only doctor, Alistair was responsible for the health of the entire community. As well as that, there were the unknown passengers of a light plane found crashed just south of town. People were missing, and the signs were that they were badly hurt. To leave was impossible.

But Sarah…

Sarah was here?

He'd requested extra police, trackers and medical back-up. Real help. It hadn't been forthcoming. There'd be someone sent from the aviation authority to check the crash site, he'd been told, but a request for additional assistance had been refused. The authorities had decided there was no evidence to justify sending such expensive help.

The decision had left him angry. He couldn't understand why the pilot had died. He was sure the blood in the cargo area wasn't the pilot's. He'd asked again, with more force.

And they'd sent Sarah.

'Hi.' She was beaming, as if she was really pleased to see him. That concept was crazy—but she was certainly beaming. She smiled brightly at him, and then she smiled at the pilot of the plane that had brought her here. She smiled her gorgeous wide smile at the luggage carrier and he smiled right back.

She beamed at everyone and they were all totally transfixed.

Well, why wouldn't they be? She was just the same as she always had been. Sarah. Five feet two in her stockinged feet and petite in every aspect.

Sarah's diminutive appearance had never stopped her making an impact. Her auburn hair floated around her shoulders in a riot of curls. Her perpetually twinkling green eyes were huge. Her rosebud mouth complemented a cute snub nose with just the perfect amount of freckles. She wore—she'd always worn—short, short skirts and shiny, frivolous shoes. Gorgeous shoes. The spotted and high-heeled footwear she wore now was bright crimson to match her neat little business suit.

She might be wearing a business suit but she didn't look corporate. Not in the least. She looked...

She looked like Sarah.

Alistair felt his gut clench in disbelief. And something else. Something he didn't want to examine.

'Aren't you going to say hi?' She was grasping his hand as if nothing lay between them. No history at all. Her smile said that maybe they were even old friends. His fingers automatically curved around her small soft hand and then, catching his breath in incredulity that this could possibly be happening, he released her and took an instinctive step back.

'What do you think you're doing here?' As a greeting it needed some finesse, he conceded, but if he was poleaxed he might as well sound poleaxed.

'I'm on the police force. I'm the forensic pathologist you requested.' She was still smiling. Maybe he was imagining it, but he thought suddenly, Her smile is forced. She's as shocked as I am.

She couldn't be. Sarah was never shocked. She was a woman in charge of her world. She danced through life as if it was hers for the taking, leaving a wave of destruction behind her.

'You're supposed to be a paediatrician,' he told her—which was also a stupid and definitely ungracious thing to say, but Sarah's smile stayed determinedly fixed.

'You haven't seen me for six years, Alistair. I've changed direction.'

'From paediatrics to forensic pathology?'

'It's a quieter life.'

'Quieter? In the police force?'

'Believe it or not, yes.'

He tried to think that through. Paediatrics was emotionally demanding, but police work would be anything but peaceful. And anyway, it didn't make sense. 'I can't imagine you ever wanting a quiet life,' he told her.

'People change, Alistair.' Her smile faded then, just a little, and the look she gave him was almost challenging. Then she seemed to regroup, bracing her shoulders and refixing that gorgeous smile. 'Now, what have you got for me?'

'I beg your pardon?'

'Your accident victim,' she told him with exaggerated patience. 'The pilot? I assume you haven't hauled me out to this back-of-beyond place for nothing?'

'No.' He took a deep breath and fought for control. 'You *are* the police pathologist?'

'I am. The report says you have a dead body, a crashed plane and a mystery. The local police officer sounds out of his depth and you lack the necessary expertise.'

Ouch. He felt his face tighten and he knew that she saw it.

'I mean you lack the necessary expertise in forensic medicine,' she amended, and he thought, Yeah, stick the knife in and twist. Hadn't that always been the way? Sarah and Grant, looking down their noses at the hick country doctor.

Sarah and Grant...

There was that twist of the gut again. The pain. Would it ever go away?

He didn't know. It was surely with him still. But for now he could only move forward, and he needed to do that now. He was stuck with Sarah, therefore the sooner they got rid of this mess the sooner he could be shot of her.

'Let's collect your luggage and get out of here,' he said brusquely, and she cast him an odd look and then smiled again.

'Fine by me. Let's go.'

Alistair Benn was not on Sarah's list of people she wished to work with. Or be with. Ever.

Like his twin brother, Alistair was almost stunningly good-looking. He was tall, dark and tanned, with crinkly brown eyes that spoke of constant laughter, a wide, white smile and a body to die for. Once upon a time Sarah had fallen deeply in love with this smile, with this body. But now... If Sarah could have named all the people she'd least like to see, then Alistair was right on top of her list.

I can't imagine you ever wanting a quiet life...

Alistair's words rang in her ears as she sat in the passenger side of his big four-wheel drive Land Cruiser and headed into town. She risked a glance across at him. His face was set and stern. Judgemental.

He'd always been judgemental, she thought. 'A moralising prig,' Grant had called him, and it had only been when Grant's excesses became painfully obvious that she'd thought: maybe Alistair had his reasons.

But he'd been so harsh.

The last time she'd seen him had been at Grant's funeral. Alistair's twin brother. She'd just been released from hospital that morning, and there'd been no time to see Grant's family before the service. Even if she had, there would have been no words to explain the unexplainable. So she'd simply appeared. She'd been distraught, aching with grief for a wasted life, desperately uncertain about the path she'd taken, and racked with guilt. Alistair had been there—of course—supporting his parents, who were so grief-stricken they'd barely been able to stand.

She'd started to approach them, moving awkwardly on crutches. She'd got within five or six feet of where they'd been grouped around the open grave, and Alistair's words had cut through her grief like a lash against raw skin.

'We don't wish to see you, Sarah. Can you leave my parents alone?'

He'd blamed her. They all had. Those six eyes, staring at her, with the loss of their loved son and brother etched hard in their faces. She'd stared at Alistair and she'd seen Grant—and the pain had threatened to overwhelm her. Alistair and Grant were identical twins. Had been identical twins. But now one was dead and one was left to haunt her for ever. She'd almost collapsed right then, but somehow she'd held on. She'd maintained her dignity—just—but she'd stumbled away as if physically struck.

She hadn't seen them since.

'Do you know what's happened here?'

Alistair was speaking to her. She flinched at the harshness in his voice, but somehow she managed to haul herself back to the present. It was a mile's drive into the township. Alistair's face was set in lines of shock and anger, and she knew he was finding this forced intimacy as impossible as she was. He was staring at the road ahead—not at her.

It was late afternoon and the sun was casting long and eerie shadows along the track. The sun's rays were deflected by the spindly gums that lined the road. A rock wallaby appeared suddenly from the undergrowth. The tiny creature stared down Alistair's vehicle until Alistair slowed; the wallaby gazed at him a moment longer, as if revelling in its moment of power, and then it hopped away.

This was an amazing place, and in a different situation Sarah might well have been mesmerised by its beauty. Dolphin Cove was a tiny settlement hundreds of miles from anywhere. In Australia's barren north, it had a reputation for a soft beauty that made it famous, but it was too far from civilisation for tourists to venture. It was too far for anyone to venture.

So why was Alistair here?

Alistair. He'd asked her a question. She needed to concentrate. What had he asked? Did she know what had happened? She did. Or part of it.

'I've read a brief report. I was told that there was a plane crash here yesterday.'

'That's it.' He still wasn't looking at her, but concentrating instead on the track, as if he feared more wallabies. Which was probably reasonable. But it certainly augmented the tension.

'So what do you know?' Sarah probed, and despite the atmosphere there was no choice for him but to answer. The only way through this was to be businesslike.

'A Cessna took off from Cairns yesterday afternoon,' he told her. 'The pilot lodged a flight plan that was pretty vague. As far as the authorities have figured the plane made an unscheduled stop somewhere north of Cairns—no one's quite sure where—and then came on over to this side of the peninsula. The plane crashed into the rocks on the beach just south of the town. One of the local fishing crews saw it go down, but if they hadn't seen it then it might well never have been discovered. It's wild country out here. But they were seen. The local police sergeant took a team out—including me—and we found the pilot. Dead.'

She nodded. 'You reported that he probably wasn't killed by the crash?'

'That's the odd thing.' He shrugged, still carefully not looking at her. 'Oh, sure, he's been knocked about a bit, but it seems he tried to make a crash landing on the beach and he darn near succeeded. There's a rock sticking out from the sand that he couldn't have seen from the air. The plane's wing caught and spun the whole thing into the cliff. So the aircraft is a bit smashed up, but not completely. He must have slowed almost to a stop before he hit.'

'He's lucky it didn't burst into flames.'

'He's dead.'

Sarah caught herself. Right. You couldn't get more dead than dead. Lucky didn't come into it.

'I guess.'

'But maybe someone has been lucky,' Alistair added, and she nodded again, thinking through the brief fax from the local policeman which she'd read on the way here. The report on the blood found in the back of the plane. The reason for the rush.

'That's the bit I don't understand.'

'That's why you're here. It's why I called for help and why we're trying to move fast. The local police sergeant—the police force here consists of exactly one—has called for reinforcements and a team of locals is combing the bushland around the wreck. You see, the cargo hold's covered in blood. It looks like a massacre took place in there. But there's no one. When we arrived the plane was still cooling. The pilot was strapped into his seat, dead. Everyone else had disappeared.'

'Everyone else?'

'I'd say at least two people have bled in that plane.' He grimaced. 'But then what would I know? You're the expert.'

She hesitated. This was impossible.

If she'd known Alistair would be here then she would have asked a colleague to come in her stead, but she was here now. She had a job to do and she needed this man's co-operation.

'Alistair, we need to work together on this one.'

'We do.' His face was grim.

'So can we set aside our…past…and get to work?'

'I've never let anything get in the way of my work.'

'Well, bully for you,' she said with a sudden spurt of anger. 'So let's just keep it that way and leave the personal innuendos alone. Tell me about the pilot.'

'I don't—'

'Just tell me about the pilot,' she said, and there was suddenly a wealth of weariness in her voice that couldn't be disguised. She caught herself, hauling herself tightly together. She'd learned that Alistair Benn was the doctor in charge of the Dolphin Cove hospital only when she'd already been in the plane on her way here, and it had been too late to tell the pilot to turn around and go back. She'd seen his name in the report she was reading, and then had spent the rest of the trip schooling her features in the way she wanted him to see them. She wasn't about to drop that façade now.

No. He couldn't see her as she so often felt—so vulnerable she felt raw. She had to turn her weariness to annoyance. 'You're not about to slow this investigation down, are you?' she snapped, and watched his face tighten again.

'Of course not.'

'Then tell me everything,' she said. 'Now.'

There was another moment of tense silence. He was regrouping, too, she thought. Good. Control was the issue here. Work.

And it seemed he agreed with her as he began to speak.

'We thought it was a regular plane crash,' Alistair told her. 'But, as I said, the pilot wasn't injured badly enough to explain his death. And the blood in the rear compartment suggested someone—or more than one—had been thrown around and badly injured in the process. The rear's been set up for storage. There are no seats. No seat belts. If anyone was sitting in the back when it crashed they'll have been thrown about heavily. But there's no sign of anyone. We've had people searching for almost twenty-four hours now.'

'And the pilot?'

'That's the reason why you in particular have been called in,' he told her. 'We carried his body back to the hospital. Because I couldn't figure out how he died, I ran routine blood tests on him. I sent the samples down to the city with the mail plane last night and this morning the results came back. This

guy has a king-sized dose of heroin on board. Huge. He didn't shoot this amount up unless it was a suicide attempt.' He told her the figures and Sarah whistled.

'So maybe someone stuck a needle into him and shot him sky-high?' she said slowly. She frowned. 'Murder by overdose is common. Can you see any needle stick marks?'

'I can't. As I said, he's a bit battered. An entry may be hidden by injury. But surely no one's going to stick a needle into a pilot flying a plane, causing it to crash?'

'So maybe it crashed and then he was murdered?'

'Right.'

'You don't believe it?' she asked, and watched his face.

'Well, you're the expert. But there was no reason for the plane to crash—or not that we can see. The pilot of the mail plane had a look at the crash site before he left last night. Harry knows his stuff. He said the plane was low on fuel, but not so low that it'd crash—the low fuel levels would be the reason it didn't explode. But everything else seems to be mechanically sound. In fact, Harry reckoned he could probably haul it off the rocks, do a bit of superficial work and have her flying again.'

'But the injuries…?'

'A bit of the cliff face came through the windscreen, hitting the pilot. Not badly—just enough to give him cuts and abrasions. Maybe it was enough to make him lose consciousness, but I doubt it. That's another thing that doesn't fit with him being murdered. He hasn't shifted from where he was when the plane hit and there's nothing that would have stopped him moving. He was securely belted in. The people in the cargo hold, though… As I said, they must have been flying without seat belts.'

'So where are they? And how many?'

'We don't know. We're hoping you might be able to tell us.'

'Right.' Could she? She sat back and thought about it.

Dr Sarah Rose was good at her job. She liked it. Forensic

medicine hadn't been her first choice, but since she'd taken it on she'd found it more and more satisfying. Solving mysteries through medicine. Keeping away from people…

No. Don't go down that road.

She looked out of the Land Cruiser window at the dying light, but she wasn't seeing the scenery. Her mind was on injured people lost in the bush. People who were depending on her to solve a mystery.

She needed to concentrate on work, which was just the way she wanted it. Especially now. Especially when she wanted so badly to keep her mind from the man beside her.

'Do we know who the pilot is?'

'We have his wallet,' Alistair told her. 'There was a passport in the cockpit cabin.'

'What did that tell you?'

'His name's Jake Condor. Thirty-eight years old. Australian. He hasn't got anyone listed as a dependant. His occupation is listed as pilot. The police have enquiries out now, trying to find where he fits. But one thing we do know— according to his passport he flew in from Thailand yesterday morning on a commercial flight. He landed in Cairns. Then he must have picked up the light plane—which is a hire plane, by the way—and come on here. With a detour. His flight plan logged at Cairns airport shows he flew north almost to Cape Tribulation and then came west, but his flying time suggests he stopped somewhere on the way. Then he flew until he crashed.'

She frowned. It wasn't making much sense. It was a jigsaw with pieces scattered and pieces missing. That was how it always was at the beginning of a case, she thought, and often—too often for comfort—those missing pieces were never found. Especially when she was called in late. And here it was twenty-four hours after the event.

'Is it too late to take me out to the plane tonight?' she asked, without much hope. Her fears were confirmed.

'Yes,' he said flatly. 'It's rough country out there, and the

last section has to be done on foot. We can't go by sea because the reefs around there are too treacherous to beach a boat. That's why the fishing crew who saw the plane crash couldn't get near it to help. Rescuers had to make the trek overland and it's about a mile of rough country. We have people out there now, looking still, but they'll give up at nightfall. It's just too dangerous.'

'But there's definitely blood in the back of the plane—and the pilot was in the front?'

'Yes.'

'You didn't think to take samples?'

There was a momentary silence and Alistair's knuckles on the steering wheel tightened. Whoa… She was going to have to tread softly here.

'No,' he said at last. 'I didn't. I went with the searchers, saw the pilot was dead and the rest were missing, then got a call to say one of my old fishermen patients was having a heart attack back here. So I came back with the body. Without thinking about blood samples.'

'Alistair, you're a family doctor,' Sarah said, her voice softening a little. 'No one's expecting you to be a pathologist.'

'Yeah, but I should have thought…'

'Are you completely on your own here?'

'Yes.'

'How do you cope?'

'As you can see,' he said grimly. 'I don't very well. I don't think of blood samples.'

'Maybe if I was having a heart attack I'd want my doctor to focus on that rather than blood samples myself,' Sarah admitted. 'And there's still time to analyse them. Can we get them tonight? The searchers out there…do you think there's anything that can be brought in with blood traces on it?'

'There might be.' Alistair still sounded tense, but at least he was moving on. He glanced at the clock on the dashboard. 'If I radio now I'll catch the search team before they call the search off for the night. But it'll be a couple of hours before they're back in town.'

'Then I'll look at the pilot first,' she said. 'And—given the fact that we might have serious injuries on our hands and missing people—let's do it now.'

Dolphin Cove Hospital was lovely. The tiny settlement had grown wealthy from pearl fishing in the previous century, and the pearl fishers had looked after their own. They'd endowed a fantastic little hospital that was envied all round the country—by those who knew about it.

In truth, no one much knew about it. Sarah gazed in astonishment at the wide verandas, with windows looking out through the palms to the beach beyond. She hadn't known this place existed.

'So this is why you came,' she whispered, staring around her with increasing delight. The sun was hanging on the horizon, a crimson ball casting a soft pink tinge over the whitewashed hospital. Every window in the place was wide open, and soft white curtains fluttered outward in the breeze. Dinner was being served on the verandas—all mobile patients were outside eating their meal while they watched the sun set over the harbour.

It was truly spectacular. The land between the hospital and the sea was a mass of palm trees, with coconuts hanging in enticing bunches. Closer to the building were frangipani, their creamy yellow flowers spreading a perfume that could be smelled from where she stood.

Out on the water there were pelicans flying low—sweeping in to land, then paddling back and forth in elegant sail-pasts, for all the world like organised flotillas of luxury liners. There were currawongs carolling in the jacarandas overhead, and a host of brilliant lorikeets were stripping a brilliant scarlet bougainvillea.

It was…magic.

'How long have you been here?' she whispered, her face reflecting her delight.

'Five years.' The set look on Alistair's face should have stopped her right there, but minding her own business had never been Sarah's strong point. Heaven knew, she'd intended to stay impersonal, but before she could stop herself the question was out.

'Since your mother died?'

Whoa. Wrong thing to say. It meant all sorts of things. It told Alistair that Sarah had kept tabs—knew what had happened to the old couple after they'd buried their son. Old Doug Benn had suffered a massive stroke only three weeks after Grant died. He'd died almost immediately, and his wife had simply faded until her death twelve months later.

'As you say.' Alistair's anger was palpable. He climbed from the Land Cruiser and she could see it was all he could do not to slam the door. 'The local policeman—Barry—is out with the searchers. I'll introduce you to him later. Meanwhile can I show you to your quarters? Do you want dinner?'

'I want to see the pilot first,' she told him. 'I'm here because this case is urgent. Let's treat it like that.'

'Fine by me.'

The morgue was at the rear of the hospital, but even the morgue wasn't an unpleasant place to be. The high windows were open and the sound of the sea pervaded—the wash of surf from around the headland. Smells in morgues were unmistakeable and unavoidable, but the salt air was giving the antiseptic, clinical morgue atmosphere a run for its money.

'Do you want to change your clothes?' Alistair asked shortly, and Sarah shook her head.

'Let me see him first. Then I'll put on overalls.'

'Fine.' They were being scrupulously polite. Alistair cast her a glance that said he still didn't really believe she was a pathologist, but he walked forward and pulled out the drawer containing the body.

Sarah didn't move. She'd learned not to.

Her first task was to stand back and get an overall impression. Things were easier that way. If you glanced at someone you got an initial impression that might be superseded later by close examining. But often that impression was right. Age. Background. Where he'd fitted into life.

Jake Condor, his passport said. Aged thirty-eight. That fitted. He looked thirty-eight.

He looked like a schmuck.

He was a pilot, but he didn't look anything like the pilot she'd just flown with on the way here. He was dressed in blue jeans, with elastic-sided boots that shone with almost astonishing brightness. His jeans were of the far-too-tight variety—designed for maximum impact on the opposite sex. Jeans like that never had the desired effect, Sarah thought, but she knew plenty of guys who wore them. They were the sort of guy who'd try to pick you up and react with total disbelief when turned down.

It was a lot to extrapolate from one pair of jeans, but Sarah was accustomed to forming impressions fast. Sometimes those impressions helped.

What else? A T-shirt with a slogan on it for some Thai beer. Interesting. That T-shirt had definitely come from overseas and it looked new. It fitted with what she'd been told.

The man had tattoos running down arms that were a bit too thin. His arms had been brawny when the tattoos had been applied, she thought. That dragon had definitely shrunk.

He was wearing a Rolex watch. Real? Maybe.

He was wearing something else that caught her attention. She walked around the table to see the leather pouch attached to his belt and glanced back at Alistair. 'It looks like a gun holster. Was there a gun?'

'No. We looked. When we saw the holster Barry did a thorough search of the plane, but there was nothing.'

'You did check the body for bullet holes?'

'We checked,' he said wryly. 'It seemed sensible.'

She nodded, moving on. The man was clean-shaven. Deeply tanned. A bit…oily, she thought. She walked forward and sniffed and was rewarded by the scent of cheap after-shave.

And his hair… His hair was horrid. It was long, black, and curling in oily strands to his shoulders. It looked as if it had been hauled back in a too tight ponytail and then released. Maybe that had happened in the accident?

His hairline was receding. Balding with a ponytail. Not Sarah's favourite look.

'He looks like a right Casanova,' Alistair said, and she glanced up at him again, surprised in a way that he was still here. Work had the capacity to block out all else. It had always been that way and was her saving grace.

A right Casanova. Yeah. 'You have that impression, too?'

'He looks a type.'

'We learn not to make judgements,' she said, in a voice that was too prim, and she surprised a smile out of him.

'I thought your job was all about judgements.'

'In the face of evidence.' She moved so she could see the man's face from both sides. 'That bump didn't kill him.'

'I wouldn't have thought so. He looks like he's got a broken nose. The guys who reached the plane first wiped him off, trying to see if there was any sign of life, but it's bled.'

She glanced down at the T-shirt and nodded. The beer slogan was spattered. Okay. He'd been hit on the nose in the crash and then he bled. It meant that he'd still been alive when the plane hit. She looked more closely at the nose. Surely after a bump like that it should have bled more?

It wouldn't have bled if the heart had stopped pumping. Death must have been fast.

'Mmm.' She wasn't moving him—still simply looking. 'Is there any damage to the back of his head?'

'Not that I can see. I had a good look when we put him on the stretcher to bring him in.'

'And you said there are no needle tracks?' She was looking

closely now at the man's forearms. Not touching. Just looking. 'If he was a user he'd have signs.'

'I didn't find syringe marks, though they wouldn't necessarily be obvious if he had only an occasional hit.'

'That makes less sense. An occasional user taking that amount when he was in control of the plane? He'd have to have been suicidal.' She stared down at the man on the table and came to a decision. Pushing her curls back from her face, she straightened. Moved right into work mode. 'Do you have a decent camera?' she asked. 'One that can do close-ups?'

'Yes.'

'Then can you show me where to change and then fetch the camera while I prepare?' she asked. 'I want to go in.'

'You mean, perform an autopsy? Here?'

'I know it's not perfect,' she told him. 'I'd far rather take him back to Cairns and do it where I have specialist equipment. But I do know how to do an autopsy without destroying evidence, and if you're willing to stay present all the time and document as I go then I'll do it now.'

'Why?'

'Because why he died will be tied up with the missing people,' she told him. 'It has to be. If there's injured people missing we may well be running out of time, Alistair. I assume that's why you called me in instead of sending the body out? I agree. It's important. So let's move.'

He gazed at her and she gazed back, unflinching. She was right and he knew it.

There was nothing for it.

He moved.

It had been years since Alistair had performed an autopsy. If there was a coroner's inquest required, Dolphin Cove's deceased were generally moved to Cairns for examination, which suited Alistair fine. He didn't miss the experience one bit. This community was tight knit, the line between patient and friend in this remote place always blurred, and to do an autopsy on a friend was unthinkable.

But back in basic training he'd learned to do them. He knew the rules, which were even more important if there was a hint of foul play. Still, he was more than happy to let Sarah take centre stage. She knew her stuff and, dressed for work, looked every bit the efficient pathologist. Enveloped in white overalls and white rubber boots, with her flaming hair tucked tightly under a surgical cap and her face masked for good measure, she almost wasn't Sarah.

Only those speaking eyes stayed with him. Alistair operated the camera and took notes as she dictated, moving with Sarah every step of the way, but he was so aware of those eyes…

Where had she learned these skills?

Why had she decided on pathology?

What a waste, he thought suddenly, remembering how he'd first seen her. She'd been at the huge city children's hospital, where she'd started her paediatric training.

'Go and say hi to Sarah if you're in the vicinity,' Grant had told him. 'After all, we're almost family. Or I hope we will be.'

So he had. He'd walked into the ward and seen her on the floor with a toddler. The bed-card—that and the ward he'd entered—had told him the little boy was suffering from leukaemia, a treatable illness in children and with a reasonable cure rate, but the treatment was just plain cruel. The little boy Sarah had been holding was bald and emaciated, and strung up to every conceivable form of tubing and monitor. He'd seemed the sort of child it was impossible to touch without hurting.

But Sarah had been touching. She'd had him in her arms, playing at being a crab. Playing at crawling—slithering over the shiny linoleum of the ward floor. Clutching the little boy in her arms and lying flat on her back, she'd been using her legs not only to manoeuvre the drip stand but to sweep them both around the floor. As they had giggled in tandem, it had

been hard to say who was the most delighted—the child or
Sarah. The little girl in the next bed had been almost pop-
eyed with jealous delight.

Alistair had watched, stunned. Sarah had had no dignity at
all. Nor had she cared. Her white pants and surgical coat had
gathered dust as she swept the floor but she hadn't seemed to
notice. When she'd looked up and found Alistair looking
down at them she'd reacted first with astonishment that he'd
looked so like Grant, and then with delight.

'See, Jonathon? We have an audience. Maybe we can organise a race? What do you say, Dr Benn? Will you be another crab? Choose a crab name immediately. Our crab name
is Horace. Kylie's in the next bed and she needs a crab car-
riage as well, so bring her down here. Don't just stand there.
Come and race us.'

What could he have said? He'd come to town for a conference, he'd been wearing a suit and tie, but in two minutes
she'd had him labelled Henrietta Crab. He'd spent the next
half-hour crab-racing, with three-year-old Kylie from the next
bed perched on his stomach and close to hysterical with glee.

He'd gone home with aching shoulder muscles, still grinning, and thinking that for once Grant had made a decidedly
good call.

That initial impression had deepened.

Grant had brought Sarah home for Christmas that year.
She'd spent a week on the farm and she'd made them all
laugh. Grant had needed to leave—of course—but Sarah had
stayed on and she and Alistair had spent the week helping his
elderly father harvest the hay. And at the end of the week
Alistair had come close to believing he was in love himself.
Dangerously close.

But that had been before. Before…

Don't think about that, he told himself fiercely. Think instead about why on earth she made the change from paediatrics to pathology.

Maybe it was pathology he needed to focus on.

'Take a shot of his fingernails,' she told him. She was lifting the dead man's hands, inspecting them with care and holding them so he could photograph. 'There's nothing here. This guy is a serious groomer. Not only does he slick his hair, he files his nails. I want a photograph of both hands, close up. It's important to establish that there's no sign of any struggle. If anyone murdered him they must have done it while he was unconscious. There's nothing to suggest that sort of injury anywhere.'

She stood back and looked again, still assessing. She'd carefully removed the man's clothes, and what they had was a five-feet-eight-inch thin male, fussy dresser, clean, well-groomed, tanned above the collar and sleeves but white elsewhere.

'I'm going to do the autopsy now,' she told him. 'You got a strong stomach? You know everything has to be witnessed and double-checked?'

'I can do it.'

'Yeah, well get me another witness before you pass out,' she told him. 'I don't want this stuffed for lack of professionalism.'

'Just do it.'

And fifteen minutes later they had their answer. Sarah was examining the contents of the man's colon with increasing incredulity.

'I've read about this,' she said. 'One of my colleagues found it once and I thought—given the amount of heroin in his blood—it had to be something similar. But to try and fly a plane…'

'What?' Alistair said, and she cast him a glance that said she'd almost forgotten he was there.

'Condoms.'

'Condoms?'

'Look. I need these photographed.' She winced and he could see the look of distaste behind the mask. 'The man's a serious twit. He's come from Thailand, right? Well, he's come bearing drugs. Drugs are still possible to obtain up in the border areas, only Customs are tight, both here and in the major Thai cities. If he's caught over there it's the death penalty, and the jail term here is pretty much equivalent. But the money is amazing. The street value of what we have here is in the tens of thousands. So Jake here has decided to go down a road that many have tried before. He packs condoms with heroin and he swallows them.'

Alistair flinched. He leaned forward and angled the camera, disbelief warring with nausea. 'How many condoms? The man must have been a lunatic.'

'It'll only work if you get rid of them fast,' Sarah said thoughtfully. 'The digestive process wears away at the rubber. This guy's eaten too many for his system to cope with. I'd imagine we're looking at a constipating of his whole system. So he arrives in the country, maybe worried that he's not passed them. He'll be in increasing discomfort, maybe he'll even give himself a purge—which might well make everything worse as it increases the pressure on the rubber. So he's flying a small plane with a couple or a few extra people as cargo. Somewhere up there a condom bursts. He suffers a massive overdose, and I mean massive. It's a miracle he managed to get the plane down at all.'

Alistair nodded, his face grim. As a scenario it was all too plausible—but horrid. He took the photographs they needed and then stood back from the table, trying to take it in. Crime like this—stupidity like this—wasn't in his ken. 'Anything else?' he asked, and she cast him a look that said she knew how badly he was disconcerted.

'I'll finish what I've started, but we have the answers to our questions. If you can find the local police sergeant for me I'll make a statement.'

'But the rest…the other passengers.'

'I don't have any answers there. I hope to heaven they haven't been eating the same diet, but according to you there's nothing we can do about that tonight. For now...' She compressed her lips. 'For now we have as much information as Jake's going to give us. I'll finish up here. Then dinner, and test the blood samples when they come in, and then bed. We worry tomorrow.'

Which was just fine, Alistair thought as he watched her work. But...dinner and bed? These were other things to worry about, besides missing drug-runners.

When he'd rung and asked for a forensic pathologist to be flown up he'd made an offer. 'The accommodation in town's pretty rough—the pub's not suitable, especially if whoever you send is female. But there's a spare bedroom in the doctor's quarters.'

The doctor's quarters. His quarters. Dinner and bed might end up being very strained indeed.

It couldn't be helped. They had missing bodies. Crime. Mystery. Personal drama had to take a back seat.

CHAPTER TWO

THE doctor's quarters were comfortably furnished and as beautiful as everything else around this place. Sarah was given time to explore them fully. Alistair led her around to the far side of the hospital, ushered her into the spare room, and then excused himself.

'I have ward rounds to do before dinner,' he told her. 'Mrs Granson will have left us a casserole in the oven. If you get hungry before I get back, go ahead. Please.'

She was left in no doubt he'd prefer not to eat with her. Which was fine. That was the way she wanted it, too. Wasn't it?

Uncertain, though, she took a long shower, soaking off the grime of the plane journey and the memory of the autopsy. Then she hauled on a soft pink leisure suit—a cross between day-dress and pyjamas—and explored Alistair's domain.

It was simple, but gorgeous. There was one vast living area, with an expansive kitchenette at one end and two bedrooms leading off the other. All the rooms opened out to the beach beyond. The hospital and associated buildings had been built in a vast line, so every room could soak in the sea.

It was still too warm for comfort. The windows, though, were wide open, and the sounds of the sea were everywhere. Sarah prowled around the little apartment, trying to figure out whether to eat or not.

She wasn't hungry.

She opened the French windows onto the veranda. A small nondescript terrier, black and white, with one leg seemingly weaker than the rest and a big black patch around one eye, roused himself from an ancient settee where he'd been snoozing. He welcomed her with total politeness and then walked definitely into the room she'd just come from—as if to say, Well, you're welcome, and I'm very grateful that you're useful. Thank you for opening the door for me.

'I hope you belong to Alistair,' Sarah said doubtfully, and then grinned as the little dog stalked straight to the refrigerator and wagged his tail. Okay, he belonged.

But it still didn't fit. Nothing seemed right about this, she thought, and the long-set-aside confusion came flooding back. Grant would never have been seen dead with a dog like this, and as far as she was concerned Alistair had higher standards than Grant.

But Grant had told her that. And Grant…

Grant had been nothing but a liar.

There was a stack of bookshelves lining the far wall and she turned her attention from the little dog's pleading eyes—and tail—to the shelves. Alistair lived to read, she remembered Grant saying. She also remembered Grant had teased him about it. 'I live life,' he'd told her. 'Alistair reads about it.'

Yeah, right.

So many things she didn't understand. So many things she'd got wrong.

She fingered the books and then moved on.

On one shelf there was a photograph in a simple wooden frame. It was all alone, as if the owner of this place didn't really want any memorabilia but hadn't been able to resist this one.

It was a photograph of Sheila and Doug Benn. Alistair and Grant's parents. They'd been at least twenty years older than this when Sarah had met them, she decided, but she still recognised them. They were on a beach somewhere. Dressed in old-fashioned bathing costumes, they stood arm in arm, laughing at the antics of their twin sons.

The twins looked about ten years old.

She could pick them still. They might be identical, but they'd been different even then. Grant would be the one doing the headstand, Sarah thought, looking at the photograph of her ex-fiancé grinning widely at the camera from upside down. Alistair was smiling down at him.

They were all smiling at Grant. That would have pleased him, Sarah thought, picking up the frame and fingering Grant's face. Grant had always had to be the centre of attention.

'Will you leave my things alone?'

She nearly dropped the photograph. She hadn't heard him come in. She whirled and Alistair was standing in the doorway, his face forbidding.

'I'm...I'm sorry.'

'I'd imagine you have photos of your own.'

'I do.' She put the photograph back on the shelf so fast that it fell face down. Then she had to adjust it, and her colour mounted all the time. 'I didn't mean to pry.'

He stared at her for a long moment—but then he shrugged. Whatever he'd wanted to say had clearly been deemed not worth the effort.

'Okay.' He took a deep breath and seemed to come to some sort of decision. 'Look, we're both stuck with this. Just...we need to keep the whole thing impersonal.'

'That's fine by me,' she managed, and he nodded.

'Have you eaten?'

'No.'

'Why not?'

'I thought I'd wait for you.'

'Muriel's casseroles don't improve with keeping.' He crossed to the kitchenette and hauled two plates out of the cupboard to lay them on the bench. Then he looked down to where the little terrier was rubbing himself ecstatically on his ankle. He smiled.

'How about you, Flotsam?' he asked the little dog. 'Has she fed you?'

'She being the cat's mother?' Sarah snapped before she

could stop herself, and Alistair's smile widened. It was a great smile, Sarah thought wistfully. A killer smile.

It would never be directed at her.

'She said it, not me,' he told Flotsam. 'The cat's mother, eh?'

But Sarah was distracted. 'Um… Flotsam?'

'Because of the way I found him. Flotsam and jetsam—washed up on the beach. I haven't found Jetsam yet, but I guess it'll happen.'

She was intrigued. This was so far from her preconception of Alistair that she had to probe further. 'You found him?'

'You don't think I'd go out and choose a dog like Flotsam, do you?' Alistair asked. He was concentrating on lifting the casserole from the oven, and she couldn't see his face, but she thought he sounded as if he was smiling. That'd make a change.

'I guess I didn't think that.' She stooped and fondled the dog's scruffy ears, and he reached out a scratchy tongue and licked the back of her hand. He was a seriously enchanting little mutt. No, she hadn't thought he'd choose a dog like this. But neither had she thought a man like Alistair would have a dog like this foisted on him. Or a man like Grant.

She needed to separate the two. Desperately.

'So how did you find him?' she managed.

'He was washed up after a storm,' Alistair told her, seeming not to notice her discomfort. 'There was a cyclone here a few months back. A boat was smashed up on the rocks. Indonesian. A couple of sailors were injured and ended up in hospital. The cargo was fish. We suspect it was taken illegally from Australian waters. Anyway, I walked down to the beach a day after the storm and the smell was unbelievable. Tons and tons of tuna, swept up on the beach and left to rot. Our local fisheries officer was taking photographs as evidence, and while he was photographing a pile of fish, the pile moved.'

'It moved?' Sarah was still rubbing the little dog's ears. Flotsam looked up at her with eyes that said, Oh, isn't this the most pathetic story—rub me some more! 'You mean—Flotsam was underneath?'

'He was crushed under a load of rotten fish. Heaven knows how he managed to survive. At that stage the boat had been broken up for forty-eight hours. Anyway, Flotsam's leg was badly broken and he was barely alive, but I hauled off a fish and he looked at me...'

'With his patched eye?'

'It's a great eye,' Alistair said, and there was no doubting the genuine affection in his voice as he looked at the little dog—who was rubbing himself round and round Sarah's hand so every inch of his scruffy little head was covered. 'Sam—the fisheries officer—said he was probably an Indonesian dog, was breaking all sorts of immigration laws by being here, and would have to be quarantined for six months if he was to stay. The best thing would be to put him down. But still that crazy eye looked at me. So I went back to the hospital and asked the wounded sailors if they knew him. They all swore they knew nothing about a dog. By the time I returned the eye had worked on Sam as well. So Sam and I declared him officially an Australian dog who'd obviously been walking along the beach minding his own business when two tons of tuna landed on his head.'

Sarah stared—and then choked. 'Oh, of course. That's the obvious thing to think, isn't it?'

'It was the obvious thing to think if we didn't want to put him down,' Alistair told her, deadpan. 'Anyway, we treated his leg—and a tricky little piece of surgery it was, too. Broken tib and fib with resultant complications. Then he had to stay here in these quarters just in case quarantine was called for, and afterwards...'

'You couldn't get rid of him,' Sarah said on a note of something akin to amazement, and Alistair scooped casserole onto three plates and managed a rueful smile.

'See? I'm not always the evil twin. And as for putting him down...could you?'

'No.' She looked doubtfully at the dinner plates. And then at Flotsam, whose short, stumpy tail was doing helicopter rotations.

I'm not always the evil twin.

Did he know what Grant used to say about him?

It didn't matter. Not any more. She had a job to do here, and a little dog to concentrate on to break the tension. 'Does he sit up at the dinner table, too?'

'He's fussy who he dines with,' Alistair said ambiguously, and carried the dog's plate through the screen door out to the veranda. He set it down on the step while Sarah watched through the screen. 'Here, mate—you can eat in privacy out here.'

Sarah stared. And felt her anger build. Whew. There was only one way to meet this hostility, she decided. Head-on. 'Are you suggesting you'd rather eat out there, too?' she demanded, and Alistair appeared to think about it.

'Maybe. But I'm hungry. I'll eat fast.'

'Meaning you want as little contamination from me as possible?'

'You said it, not me, lady,' Alistair told her. 'But let's just leave it there.'

The silence was deafening. They ate, and the tension was growing all the time. Sarah stirred the casserole—which was some sort of indiscriminate stew—and wished she could be anywhere but here.

One mistake…

No. It had been more than one mistake. She'd been hauled into Grant's world. She'd been caught in the bright bubble of laughter and excitement and sheer buzz, and she hadn't looked below the surface until it was far, far too late.

She'd met his family.

She remembered the night Grant had given her the engagement ring. He'd taken her up to the top of the Rialto Tower in Melbourne, where the lights of all the world had spread out beneath them.

'Now, when all the world is at our feet, I'm at your feet,' he'd told her, and he'd knelt and given her the most exquisite diamond.

The moment had been something out of a fairytale. It had seemed…fantastic. But she'd looked down at that gorgeous laughing face and she'd felt a stir of disquiet. It had happened so fast—it had been as if they were playacting. Was there any substance there?

But she'd accepted. Of course she'd accepted. He had to be special. After that wonderful Christmas she'd wanted so much to be a part of his world. So she'd worn his ring, and she'd loved him and laughed at his jokes and been carried along in his world, until reality had finally hit and she'd seen what really lay beneath. And she'd realised the real reason she'd agreed to marry Grant.

Loving one twin was no basis for marriage to another.

Crazy thought. It was a crazy time, long past. She needed to focus on now. On what Alistair was saying.

'You don't wear his ring.'

Alistair was watching her from the other side of the table. His voice was carefully neutral—neither approving nor disapproving.

'I thought you wanted to stay impersonal.'

'So I do.' His eyes stayed calm—watchful and appraising. 'But I'm still wondering.'

'I'm not in another relationship, if that's what you mean,' she told him. 'But, no, I'm not still pining for Grant. I've moved on. Don't you think it's time you did, too?'

'I don't think you can move on from Grant.'

'He'd have liked to hear you say that,' she said, and there was no way she could keep the note of bitterness from her voice. 'He had us all dancing from his strings. You included.'

'I never did what he wanted.'

'No, but you judged on his behalf.'

'You killed him.'

It was like a punch to the face. Dear God…

She took a great lungful of air and it wasn't enough. She found her eyes filling. Numbly, blindly, she stood.

What had she told him? That she'd moved on?

She'd done no such thing. The pain was right there, waiting to slam back. And it slammed back now.

She was *not* going to let this man see her cry.

'Are…are the blood samples here yet?' she whispered, turning away so he couldn't see her face. Taking her plate to the sink. Avoiding his gaze.

'Not yet.' The brief flash of fury had faded. There was a trace of something else in his voice now. Confusion? She didn't know. She couldn't care. 'They won't be here until the searchers return to town.'

'When will they be back?' she managed.

'Any time. I'd assumed they'd be in by now.'

'Then I'll wait in my bedroom,' she told him. 'Thank you for dinner. It was better than the company. Let me know when the blood samples arrive.'

Enough. Her voice wobbled dangerously and she turned before the first tear could fall. She was moving out through the door before he could speak.

'Sarah…' It was a tentative call of her name. He sounded unsure. Concerned.

But she didn't turn. She couldn't. She had to get out of here right now.

As Alistair cleared up the casserole he swore. Over and over again. What was going on here? What had Sarah said? That the casserole was better than the company.

Maybe she was right.

He really had to do something about Mrs Granson's house-keeping, he told himself, in a vain attempt to distract himself from what was really important. The casserole was disgusting.

Right. The casserole was disgusting. Which made him… what? Even more disgusting?

No. He refused to accept judgement from someone like Sarah. What right did she have to criticise?

What right did she have to look as she did? As if he'd struck her—hard.

He thought suddenly of that last time he'd seen her. At the cemetery as they'd buried Grant. His parents had been inconsolable. And Sarah had appeared, wobbling on crutches, looking pathetic. She'd even tried to smile.

He'd been so…wild! Wild with grief at such an appalling waste. Such an appalling loss. At what had seemed such an ultimate betrayal of how he and his parents had felt about her.

So he'd pushed her away with his hurtful words and she'd looked just as she looked now. Like a wounded animal who'd been hurt even unto death.

Six years ago, standing beside his brother's open grave, he'd felt an almost unbearable urge to recant. To take back what had been said. To follow her and take her into his arms.

He hadn't done it then and he was darned if he'd do it now. But once again that urge was there.

What right did she have to look so wounded?

At his feet, Flotsam was gazing up at him, a worried look on his scraggy little face, and Alistair abandoned the clearing up, scooped the pup into his arms and took him out onto the veranda. The sea always had the capacity to soothe him. Maybe it could tonight.

He sat on the back step and Flotsam kept right on looking at him. Was he imagining it, or was there reproach in the little dog's eyes?

'Don't look at me like that,' he told him. 'She killed my twin.'

Flotsam cocked one ear and kept on looking. Explain, his look said. Or maybe his look didn't say any such thing, but Alistair needed to explain it to himself, to go over the whole thing one more time.

As he'd gone over it thousands of times before.

'They were drunk,' Alistair said wearily. 'Or rather Grant was drunk. He used to party heavily. And drive fast. All the time. Not like you and me, mate, with our nice sensible truck. Grant had a Ferrari, and he and Sarah used to speed around the town looking like something out of *Who* Magazine. Heaven help you if you got in Grant's way. What he wanted he got. And Sarah…she was so desirable. Everyone loved Sarah. Everyone. Because of her father she was famous. She had money, looks—everything. That's why Grant wanted her—why he wanted to marry her when he'd never shown any sign of marrying any other woman in his past—and there were plenty of those.'

He was being sidetracked. Flotsam was giving him a sideways look, as if this wasn't explaining anything. Which it wasn't.

'Okay. Cut to the chase. She drove his car,' Alistair said heavily. 'Sure, she was under the legal alcohol limit, but she was on drugs. Sedatives, uppers, downers—I don't know exactly what. They must have been legal prescriptive drugs or she would have been charged, but it doesn't matter. Grant used to use them, too. I thought…we hoped Sarah might influence him. Stop him using them. But, no, it seems she was just as bad as he was. So he was drunk and she was drugged. And she drove him home in that damned car. Not over the legal limit, but too fast for the icy road they were travelling. They were showing off, the pair of them, and they crashed.'

Flotsam was looking worried now, as well he might. There was such anger in Alistair's voice. Such unresolved fury.

'Of course they crashed,' Alistair continued, his fury fading to a deadly weariness which was almost worse. 'And Grant died. I can't tell you what that feels like, can I, Flots? You'd need to be a twin to know. Grant and I…we didn't get on, but he was my twin. Part of me. I can't get away from that. And she killed him. She had concussion and lacerations and Grant got death. The driver's side of the car—her side—was hardly touched. Even at the end she veered so that *she* wouldn't cop the impact. But Grant would. Grant did. Grant got death. He had an unstable neck fracture which wasn't picked up and the day after the accident he died in his sleep. It killed my parents. You have no idea, Flots. You have no idea…'

Silence. Flotsam seemed to take in the enormity of what he'd been told. The little dog stirred in his arms, reached up and licked him, nose to chin.

'Gee, thanks. A kiss better.' He grimaced. 'It doesn't help.'

He sat on, the dog in his arms, staring out to sea. Was she sleeping? he thought. He shouldn't care.

He did care.

Why had she looked like that?

It was a life skill, he thought savagely. Manipulating. She'd manipulate people as Grant had manipulated people.

The phone rang indoors and Alistair almost welcomed it. Work. Work had been his salvation in those first months after Grant died. It had been a long time since he'd felt like that. He'd grieved for Grant but he'd moved on. He'd built himself the life that he'd always wanted—as a family doctor in a community that depended on him. He had fun. He dated. He knew what he wanted from life.

Or did he?

Suddenly she was here and his whole life was tumbling about him. It'd be transitory, he told himself. Tomorrow or the next day this mystery would be cleared up and she'd be out of here. His life could resume.

Only…

Go and answer the phone, he told himself. For heaven's sake get back to work. Leave this pain alone.

Easy to say. Impossible to do.

Sarah was reading the report for the fourth time when Alistair knocked on her bedroom door, and she was almost glad of the interruption. If she'd known it was anyone but Alistair she'd have been delighted. She was climbing walls.

How could he make her feel like this? How could he have the capacity to tear her apart all over again?'

Maybe because she'd never healed in the first place.

'Damn him,' she whispered. 'Damn them all. I don't need any of them. I'm fine by myself and I always will be. Alistair Benn can condemn me all he likes and it doesn't affect me.'

Liar.

'The searchers have come back,' Alistair called. 'They haven't found anything but you might like to talk to the police sergeant in charge of the case.'

Of course she would. She'd like to talk to anyone but Alistair.

At least now there was work to do.

There'd been a tarpaulin on the floor of the cargo area and it was heavily bloodstained. Maybe there was enough here to work with, Sarah thought, as one of the men unfolded it for her. The blood shouldn't have soaked in so far that she couldn't retrieve enough to put under a slide.

The first and the most imperative medical procedure, however, was to attend to one of the team. Despite having found no one, they'd come back with a patient.

Don Fairlie, the local publican, was about sixty pounds overweight. He was supported by a mate, and by the look of exhaustion on his mate's face it was lucky Alistair didn't have another heart attack on his hands. As Sarah and Alistair entered the emergency department Don was groaning in pain and looking sick.

'He tried to do some rock-hopping,' the local police sergeant told them.

Barry. Dolphin Cove's only policeman.

Barry Watkins needed no introduction as the representative of the law. A big man, he was muscled rather than pudgy, with the shirt of his police uniform stretched far too tight across his barrelled chest. His close-cropped hair was cut to look deliberately macho and he stood with the aggressive stance of a male who was ready for anything. Sarah recognised this stance and winced every time she saw it. To finish the whole macho image he carried a wicked-looking pistol at his hip.

Sarah, standing back as Alistair took control, thought instinctively, There's no love lost between these two.

She could soon see why.

'Bloody pansy,' Barry muttered as he stared down at Don. 'Wasting our time by breaking his arm. And we didn't find anyone. If I could have a decent search party…'

'We're operating with volunteers,' Alistair said brusquely. 'I'll get you something for the pain, Don, and we'll get you through to X-ray. Meanwhile, Barry, you might like to have a talk with Dr Rose. She's done the autopsy and has information you need.'

'I'm glad someone has.' The policeman shifted away from the publican and Sarah, casting a doubtful glance at the pallid and sick Don—did Alistair need help?—moved reluctantly with him. She had no choice. Alistair's body language said he'd like to be shot of the pair of them.

Duty decreed she had to work with this policeman, though when she outlined what she'd found in the pilot's body she discovered her reaction to the policeman was exactly the same as Alistair's. Distaste. Even dismay.

'Drug-runners.' The big man's eyes lightened and his hand went instinctively to his gun. 'You mean the people we're looking for might be serious crims?'

'If everyone aboard the plane was involved in running drugs I hardly see why the pilot needed to carry so much more in his stomach,' Sarah said mildly, but he shook his head.

'Maybe he was trying to smuggle a bit more on the side. Or maybe they were drug-runners simply paying our man to pilot the plane and he was trying to make more profit that he should. Any way you look at it they'll have drugs. That's why they'll have run. There's no other logical explanation. What's the bet they're hiding up in the hills with a planeload of drugs? They won't come out until we stop searching.'

'Whoever they are, they're wounded,' Sarah told him, and he nodded. He had to agree with her there.

'Yeah, that's right. And that's our best shot at making them break cover. They could stay for weeks up there and we won't find them. We're at the end of the wet season, so there's fresh water, and everywhere you look there's oysters.'

'Oysters make a difficult meal for wounded people,' Alistair said over his shoulder. 'They're really hard to break open. And they're hardly a balanced diet.'

'Yeah, but they'll be desperate,' Barry reasoned. 'They must be hiding something. Sound carries everywhere up there. They must know we're looking.' He fingered his gun again and Sarah winced. She had no sympathy for drug-runners, but this man made her really uneasy.

Behind her Alistair was administering morphine. She wanted to help. Increasingly she felt a compulsion to do what she'd been trained to do when things were out of control. Clear the room of everyone but patients and staff.

And as if on cue came the order. 'Can everyone leave?'

She blinked. Alistair was obviously feeling the same as she was. 'Don's hurt and he needs peace,' he said, and she could only agree.

'I need to talk to the pathologist,' Barry said, with more than a hint of belligerence.

'My report's here,' she told him. 'I talked my post mortem examination to tape. You'll need time to listen. I'll help Dr Benn with Don's arm. I'll do the testing that I can on the blood samples from the tarpaulin and then I'll give you a ring to let you know the results. Dr Benn has your phone number?'

'Yes, but—'

'She'll ring you, Barry,' Alistair said, with more than a hint of weariness. 'I need her help now. I need the room cleared.'

There was a nurse hovering in the background and he looked across at her. 'Claire, can you show everyone out? Now?'

They wheeled Don through to X-ray, then took the films into the tiny viewing room next door.

'It's just a dislocation,' Alistair said, and sounded relieved. As well he might. 'I'll give him a small dose of benzodiazepine and try and put it back. There's no need for you to stay.'

Sarah looked at the film, her head cocked on one side, considering. 'It's been dislocated for a while, and he's had to walk in a huge amount of pain. There'll be muscles tight with spasm. You'll be lucky if you can get it back.'

'I can try.'

'And I can watch,' she said softly. 'You have another doctor here, Alistair. I'm happy to help.'

Of course the shoulder couldn't be reduced. Alistair checked the X-ray again, confirming an anterior dislocation without a break. He administered more morphine and valium and waited until they took effect.

'Do it quick, Doc,' Don said, obviously gritting his teeth.

'I'll try and find a bullet for you to bite on, if you like,' Sarah told him, trying to lighten the mood for all of them. 'Having your shoulder put back after dislocation is real hero stuff. I'll watch and be ever so admiring.'

The publican gave her a wan grin. 'You mean I'm not allowed to scream?'

'Heroes never scream.' She smiled down at him, her eyes warmly sympathetic. 'But if you do, us heroines never tell. You can shout all you like and I'll never tell a soul. You can even whimper and I'll carry your awful secret to the grave.'

'You're a woman in a million,' he said, then looked up at Alistair and grimaced. 'Okay, Doc. I have my cheer squad all ready. Do your worst.'

But he couldn't. Alistair took the big man's arm firmly in

his grasp, took a deep breath, then pulled gently and firmly, downward and outward.

Nothing.

'Damn.'

'You can pull harder,' Don said bravely, and Sarah beamed at him. Yep, he definitely was hero material.

'You are so good. But Dr Benn's not going to try again. If the shoulder doesn't slip in first try then there's no use going on. The muscles will just tighten further.' She glanced up at Alistair. 'What do you reckon, then? Will we put the big boy to sleep?'

It made sense. The only thing stopping the shoulder slipping back into place was muscle spasm, and the way to stop that was to relax the muscles completely. Which meant a relaxant anaesthetic. The problem with that was that the patient had to be intubated. It was a two-doctor job.

'I don't have an anaesthetist,' Alistair said. His lips were compressed together and Sarah could see that he hated that he'd failed. It wasn't his fault, though. With such a big man, and with the amount of prolonged pain the man had been suffering, it was odds-on that no one could have reduced the dislocation.

'Who normally gives anaesthetic?' she asked.

'No one,' he said shortly. 'I send patients to Cairns.'

'And if it's urgent?'

'We die,' Don told her bluntly, before Alistair could answer. 'We're a one-doctor town. We know that. It's a risk we take.' He grimaced. 'Not that I'm intending to die, mind. And if you, miss, can give an anaesthetic, then I'd just as soon not have to wait for transport to Cairns.'

'I don't blame you.' Sarah looked across at Alistair, perturbed. This was a huge responsibility he was carrying—sole doctor with no back-up. How did he cope?

At least he didn't have to cope now, she thought. Not alone. 'I can give an anaesthetic,' she told them. 'Do you have the equipment?'

'Yes, but…' Alistair was frowning.

'Or would you prefer to give the anaesthetic while I do the manipulation? You're probably stronger, but I'm game.'

'Hey,' Don said, startled. 'Game? You make it sound like it's a *Girl's Own* adventure.'

'Of course it is,' she told him. 'Like lighting a fire by rubbing sticks. Only manipulating shoulders is much quicker. Have you eaten anything in the last few hours?'

'Not since lunchtime,' Don told them.

'Well, then.' Sarah turned to Alistair. 'Do we have what we need? Can we start? Now?'

'It'd mean he wouldn't have to fly out.' Alistair was staring at her as if she'd suddenly sprouted Martian antennae. 'The locals hate the flight to Cairns. To go there for every simple operation…'

'You should have another doctor here.'

'Oh, right. With a district population of less than two thousand and no big town facilities? You try attracting another doctor.'

'And yet you came?'

'I'm different,' he said shortly. 'I love it.'

She gazed at him thoughtfully. Grant had derided him so much—his country hick brother who was never going to amount to anything. But he *was* amounting to something. Of course he was. Who was more important? she thought suddenly. The high-earning powerful neurosurgeon in a big city hospital, or the doctor who'd made a decision to earn a tenth the amount but care intensely for a tiny community like this?

'He's another one who came by choice,' Don said. 'Like me. I love the place. Unlike our representative of the police force.'

'The locals don't get on with Barry?' she asked, and Don gave a derisory snort as though the thought was clearly ridiculous.

'He's been moved sideways against his will,' Alistair told

her, sounding unwilling to go further. But Don was only too ready to fill in the details.

'Barry was given the choice of coming here or leaving the police force,' Don said, his dislike sounding in every word. 'He was involved in a high-speed police chase a couple of years back, just outside Cairns. Two twelve-year-olds in a stolen car. It was dead clear they were kids—for heaven's sake, their heads hardly reached the top of the seat. But Barry pulled out all stops, even firing warning shots. He shot out the tyres, the kids crashed and they were killed.'

Don hesitated, and Sarah could see he was trying to balance his dislike with justice, but obviously he failed.

'I know sometimes it's a hard call for the police—whether they chase or pull out,' he said slowly. 'But what made it worse was Barry's attitude. Some reporter gave him a few drinks after the trial and Barry's on record as saying scum like that deserve everything they get.'

'Oh, no.'

'No's right,' the publican told her. 'Especially as the kids came from the most appallingly underprivileged homes. They never had a chance. Anyway, Barry managed to avoid being sacked, but he was demoted and moved to where he was least likely to do media damage. So Dolphin Cove got him. He hates being here and we'd prefer no police at all. He gives the locals a hard time. I've got a couple of alcoholics I cope with—when they get drunk on my patch I pick 'em up and take them home. But Barry enjoys tossing them into jail. They're fined, and who suffers from that? Their wives and kids—who go without anyway. And kids petrol-sniffing... Instead of giving them a clout on the ear and a lecture, Barry sends 'em to Cairns. To juvenile detention. They come back little criminals in the making. But meanwhile...' He touched his arm and grimaced. 'You're sure you can do this?'

Sarah nodded. She looked at Alistair. 'And you?'

He nodded back. He looked bemused, she thought. Out of his depth. Which was good. He'd hurt her so much. It was good to have the boot on the other foot for a change, even if it was for such a minor instance. 'If you're sure,' he told her. 'And if Don trusts a stranger.'

'She's no stranger,' Don said soundly. 'She's got the prettiest smile I've ever seen in a woman. Or in a man, either, for that matter. She looks a friend to me. So I'll lie back and think of England and let you two do your worst.'

CHAPTER THREE

THE publican's arm was harder to fix than they'd thought, though Alistair had the equipment—'In an emergency I call in the Flying Doctor for help, and I have a fully equipped theatre with all the drugs in case there's someone here to help me.'

He made everything ready as Sarah did a careful examination and took a history. To give an anaesthetic without doing both was stupid.

And that was where she found problems.

The man was seriously overweight. She listened to his chest and then quietly signalled to Alistair that she wanted to see him outside.

'I need advice,' she told him. 'That chest almost sounds asthmatic. It's scaring me. My anaesthetics is basic. I don't want him dying of a dislocated shoulder.'

'Do you want to call it off?' Alistair asked, but she shook her head and turned to the nurse.

'Claire, can you set up a phone link with the duty anaesthetist in Cairns?'

Two minutes later the anaesthetist from Cairns was on the line. He listened as she outlined the problem while Alistair watched on.

'Okay.' She asked him to repeat his instructions twice for good measure and then replaced the receiver. She thought it through. Finally she looked up at Alistair.

'I can do this,' she told them. 'Now I can. I've gone over the dosage. It's a really fast anaesthetic. We go in fast. Alistair, the advice is that if you have problems then we reverse the anaesthetic and give up—straight away—but we'll give it this one shot. The anaesthetist says we should have no problems. Once the muscles are relaxed everything should fit in easily.' Her eyes held Alistair, questioning. 'If you're okay with it?'

'Believe it or not,' he said, holding her gaze with a look that was disconcertingly direct, 'I'm more confident now than I am before you conceded you had problems.'

They started.

She injected and started intubation. The theatre was hushed apart from the gentle whoosh-whoosh of the bagged air. The big man was unconscious, every muscle slumping.

'Go,' she muttered.

Alistair gave her one last questioning look. She nodded. He took the man's arm, pulled downward, outward, twisting…

The shoulder clicked back into place.

'Well done,' Alistair said softly as she started the reversal, and she flushed.

'You mean well done for not knowing what to do?'

'No. I mean well done for admitting you were unsure before we ran into serious trouble.' He glanced up at her and smiled. 'I wouldn't have thought it of you.'

'Was I so arrogant when you knew me?'

Her tone must have sounded…sad? Wistful? She bit her lip and turned back to her dials, but she was aware that Alistair's eyes were on her.

'No,' he said softly, and his smile faded. 'No. Grant was arrogant. I just…I always group you together.'

'It must be nice to be so certain,' she said shortly, and she felt rather than saw his brows come together in confusion. 'Concentrate on your work,' she snapped.

'My work here is done,' he told her, and the confusion on his face was mirrored in his voice. 'Thanks to you.'

Finally, with the publican recovering nicely, and his wife and three of his seven kids sitting round his bedside waiting for him to wake up properly and tell them all about it, Sarah decided they were free to part. Which was what she desperately wanted.

'I need to sort these blood samples,' Sarah told him. She was still feeling discomfited. Alistair's presence—what he'd said—there was too much to ignore. She wanted him to go away so she could concentrate on her work.

But it wasn't going to happen.

'I'll help you.'

'I don't need help.'

'If it's a police case then you're going to need an independent witness to verify your findings.'

'You can look at the tarpaulin in the morning.'

'Let's do it now.'

Which made it worse. Not only was he disconcerting and upsetting, he was far too close.

Using the kit she'd brought with her, she worked with the scrapings and he was right at her shoulder. She found it so hard to concentrate it was almost impossible. But at least what she found was straightforward.

'There's been at least two bleeders,' she told him. 'I have an AB and an A blood group.' She flicked through a few more slides. 'There's a lot more of the AB.'

'So we have two people.'

'We have two people who bled. We might well have half a dozen people.'

Alistair stood back and looked down at the tarpaulin. They'd spread it out over the floor. The blood spatters were all over it.

'This isn't minor. Someone's lost a huge amount of blood.'

'So maybe they're already dead.' Sarah turned and looked down, too. It was a mute object. A tarpaulin. It should be able to speak, she thought. How had that blood appeared? Who did it belong to and where were they now?

'You'd think they'd consider their lives more important than a few bags of heroin,' Alistair said, and she knew he was thinking exactly the same thing as she was.

'Our pilot swallowed condoms full of heroin,' she whispered. 'What a risk...'

'And these people are risking everything as well. By smuggling drugs.'

'Not necessarily.' She shook her head. She'd stayed in her theatre gown but had discarded her cap. The same with Alistair. They were robed all in green. It should have helped make this more of a professional relationship—and maybe it did—but there were still undercurrents she couldn't do a thing about. 'There's something else.'

'What?'

'Why would they have flown right out here?' she asked. 'Dolphin Cove is hundreds of miles from anywhere. Let's assume they've brought back a stash of heroin from Thailand. What would they want to do with it? The answer is easy. They'd want to sell it. Fast. They might want to keep it for a while and sell it in small lots, but even so...why bring it all the way to Dolphin Cove? And were they heading *specifically* for Dolphin Cove?'

'No. At least, we don't think so. They were south of the township. They must have passed almost over our runway and then flown further.'

'But there wasn't much fuel in the tank. Their destination must have been somewhere close by. Where?'

'You're asking me?'

'I'm asking myself.' She frowned. 'We need serious police help here. I don't think Barry's going to be much use. I'll contact headquarters and see if we can get some decent people sent up.'

'There's a problem with that.'

'What?'

'It's the Commonwealth Heads Of State Conference in Brisbane starting tomorrow,' Alistair told her. 'When I was contacted to be told you were on your way, the detective who spoke to me said they've had terrorist threats. Every available policeman in the country is in Brisbane. Plus there's been a bus crash south of Cairns, which is taking resources. I doubt you'll get anyone here for at least two days. I'd imagine you would have been told that before you left.'

She had. Of course she had. She bit her lip. 'That's right. I forgot. Then these people…' She stared down at the tarpaulin, frowning in concentration. As if she could make some sort of sense of the blood patterns. She couldn't. 'If these people aren't already dead then they may well soon be.' She closed her eyes. 'Dear heaven…'

There was a long silence as they both thought through the implications. 'There's nothing we can do about it now,' Alistair said at last, his voice heavy with foreboding. 'We'll go out to the plane ourselves tomorrow, but it's no use beating ourselves about it now. It won't help.' He lifted his hand lightly to her cheek and touched her—a feather-touch. A touch of reassurance, nothing more. 'You must be exhausted. You've done too much for one day, Dr Rose. It's time you went to bed.'

'Yes. I…' She stared up at him, and before she could stop herself her hand lifted to trace the line where he'd touched her. As if he'd left some indelible mark.

Their gazes locked and held.

And stayed.

What was happening? She didn't know. Sarah found herself staring up into the eyes of this big man who was so like the man she'd once thought she loved. He was so…close.

He wasn't Grant.

And yet…and yet…

She stared up at him and her world shifted. She felt that gut-wrenching shift—the change that told her she was no longer in control. She was spinning….spinning…

And the last time that had happened to her it had ended in tragedy and death and regret for the rest of her life.

He saw it. She knew the moment he registered the horror in her eyes. His brow snapped down in concern as she took an involuntary step backward.

'Sarah…'

'Y… You're right. I need to go to bed.' Damn, there were tears behind her eyes. Tears of weakness. Tears of stupidity. 'If there's nothing else…?'

'There's nothing else.'

'Then I'll see you in the morning.'

'Goodnight, Sarah.'

She blinked. She couldn't believe the note she heard in his voice. Tenderness? Caring?

Nonsense. The Benn boys didn't do tenderness and caring. Had she learned nothing?

'Goodnight, Dr Benn,' she whispered, and it was as much as she could do to turn and walk with dignity down the corridor towards the doctor's quarters.

She wanted to run.

She woke to kisses. Not just feather-light social greetings, but long, amorous declarations of absolute devotion. Sarah opened her eyes and Flotsam was two inches away, his whole body quivering in delight. His pink tongue came out again, he launched himself forward and Sarah hauled her sheet up over her face to protect herself.

'Ugh. Horrible dog. Go away.'

Flotsam did no such thing. He quivered and quivered, and when Sarah cautiously lifted an edge of the sheet to see, the little dog dived down, right under the bedclothes, with such practice that Sarah knew he'd done it many times before.

'I'd have left you under the fish,' she said. 'Yikes! Do you mind? I happen to be ticklish.'

'Flotsam's a foot fetishist.' She looked up and Alistair was smiling down at her. He was wearing casual jeans and an open-necked khaki shirt with the sleeves rolled up. His eyes were twinkling down at her and she looked up at him and thought, Uh-oh. Here I go again.

Or did she need to go again? Had the pain ever gone away?

The Benn brothers were stunning. Amazing.

And one Benn brother was in her bedroom.

Unconsciously she hauled her sheet up to her chin—which locked Flotsam in. Flotsam did a three-sixty turn under the covers, pushed with all his might, and his nose emerged from the end of the bed. Exposing Sarah's toes.

This wasn't the most dignified position she'd ever been in, Sarah decided, and she could feel herself flushing.

'Um…do you mind removing your dog?'

'Shall I come in and get him?'

'No! Call him from there.' Flotsam's tail was beating a tattoo against her legs. His delight was infectious and his fur was definitely tickling. Sarah was feeling so far out of control she might well be drowning. Alistair was grinning down at her, her toes were sticking unceremoniously out from the covers and Flotsam was deciding to lick again.

'I'm calling you both,' Alistair told her, but the twinkle behind those lazy brown eyes told her that he knew exactly how discomfited she was. 'If you can be ready in thirty minutes we're planning on going out to the wreck. The hospital's quiet. The sickest person here is Don, and he's awake and complaining that he's only been given two rashers of bacon for breakfast so I'm not too worried. I'm releasing him forthwith. I thought I'd go out to the wreck with you. Maybe four eyes are better than two if we're looking for clues.'

She looked up at him and the twinkle had died.

'You don't trust Barry,' she said on a note of discovery, and he gave a rueful smile.

'Barry won't break any rules.'

'But he's macho?'

'If someone was running,' Alistair said carefully, 'then Barry might think any means of stopping him was okay.'

'But you weren't out there with him yesterday.'

'I had a suspected heart attack on my hands here. Les Cartier had a severe angina attack the night before last, which was why I had to come back from the wreck so fast. I didn't like to leave him yesterday, but today he's looking good.'

'But if you're needed…'

'I'm more likely to be needed out there.' He hesitated. 'To be honest, Don might look a bit of a wuss, and Barry's scathing about him, but Barry'll keep a rein on his temper when Don's around. Don runs a decent pub and he's more capable than anyone I know of calming tension. But Barry alone…'

'You don't think I could calm things down?'

'I don't think Barry would even notice you're here,' Alistair said honestly.

'You really are worried.'

'I think there are people out there who are wounded. I also agree that they must be hiding.' He hesitated. 'We were at the crash within half an hour of the plane going down. For people to be badly wounded yet wander so far they couldn't be found doesn't make sense. They should have stayed on the beach. And at night… It's pitch dark out there, but it's not so far from town that they couldn't see the glow from the lights. No. There's a problem. And I don't want Barry to find what that problem is when there's no one around to control the worst of his excesses. Jack Christy, our local mechanic, can come out mid-morning, and he's tough enough to do the same as me, but he's held up until then. Someone needs be there.'

'So you're coming with us?'

'Just for a couple of hours until Jack arrives. Now, do you want to get dressed?' He grinned suddenly. 'I'm assuming you have panties and a bra on under that sheet, but…'

She gasped. While she'd been concentrating on what Alistair was saying Flotsam had been tugging the sheet sideways. She was exposed almost to the thighs. Her legs were bare and…

She clutched. Just in time.

'Take your dog and leave,' she said, with as much dignity as she could muster.

'But you'll come with us?'

'Of course I'll come. But get out. Both of you.'

*　　*　　*

The trek to the wreck took over half an hour of rough climbing.

The cove where the plane had crashed was surrounded by wild, rock-strewn hills and rough bushland. It was tough, inhospitable country. There were better beaches closer to the town, so no one ever felt the need to go there and so there was no established track. To reach the plane they needed to bush-bash through dense countryside, and by the time they'd walked for fifteen minutes Sarah's face and arms were covered with a myriad of minor scratches.

She'd been warned and she'd come prepared. Knowing there was a plane wreck in rough terrain before she'd left the city, she'd packed sensible bushwalking gear—baggy pants, loose shirt and sensible hiking boots—but no one could escape the scratches completely. The lawyer vine that lined the track, looping its way round trees and undergrowth, had savage prickles that couldn't be avoided.

If Alistair hadn't been hiking right behind her she might have complained. But she didn't. She trudged on, aware that Barry was being condescendingly slow on her behalf. And for some reason he was also being malicious. They trekked in silence, and only Flotsam's cheerful antics as he dashed madly in front and then rushed back to ensure they were still following kept her spirits from being right down in her hiking boots.

Their party was five in total—Alistair, Sarah, Barry, and two local women who were experienced bushwalkers and were here solely for the search. There was another team already out at the cove, already searching. A light plane had been organised to comb the area as well, and they could see it working its way methodically back and forth as they walked,

'Fat lot of good that'll do, though,' Barry told them. 'These guys don't want to be found.'

'Surely if they're hurt they'll come searching for help,' Sarah said mildly. She flinched as a rock Barry had just trodden on rolled backwards under her feet. Surely he hadn't needed to dislodge it?

'No way,' Barry snapped, as if she was being thick.

'Why not?'

'They'll be hiding drugs.'

'Okay,' she conceded.

Alistair was walking behind her and she was absurdly aware of his presence—and his silence—but she had to make her mind stay on the job. She was here as an investigative pathologist, and as such she had to think through every angle, even if it did come outside her specialist medical frame of reference.

'Let's assume they did have a load of drugs as cargo,' she said thoughtfully, wincing as a branch Barry had pulled aside slapped back and hit her in the face. Barry was walking straight ahead of her and making no concessions to the fact that anyone was following. More and more she was starting to think his actions were deliberate. 'Let's assume they managed to get drugs out of the plane. Why don't they hide the drugs and then come for help? There's heaps of places here they could hide things. They can't know they'll be treated as criminals. They can't have known the pilot had a gut full of drugs—they wouldn't have been stupid enough to fly with him if they'd known.'

'It makes sense to me,' Alistair said mildly, but Barry obviously disagreed.

'Criminals are stupid,' Barry snapped, but Sarah frowned to herself as she trudged on. The jigsaw pieces weren't fitting at all, and she didn't like it.

Another rock rolled back.

Another branch hit her in the face.

'They must be dead,' Alistair said from behind her, and she knew he was thinking exactly what she was thinking. Drugs might be important, but no one would choose profit over life.

'It'd make our work a lot easier if they are,' Barry said, and Sarah winced. She really didn't like this man.

She didn't like Alistair, but she didn't like Barry more. And he was pulling another branch aside.

The man was a git.

Enough was enough. As a forensic pathologist Sarah moved in a world peopled by tough guys—criminals as well as cops—and she'd become used to holding her own. Barry might be tough, but so was she.

'Sergeant, if you let one more branch fly back and hit me in the face I'm going to have you up for assault,' she murmured, and the policeman turned around and stared at her. In his face she saw the confirmation of what she'd suspected.

She was a woman, she was a professional, and she was his superior. The combination of the three had brought out the worst of his antagonism. It wasn't worth trying to placate him, she thought ruefully. She'd worked with this type before. Placating would make her seem weak in his eyes, and it'd just make him worse.

'Sergeant, our priority is first and foremost to keep people alive,' she told him. 'Sure, we may have a crime on our hands, but right now we have one dead pilot who's smuggled a bit of heroin and died for his pains. We also have missing people who, as far as we know, have done nothing illegal. They might be dying right at this minute. That's our job, Sergeant. To find them. Alive. As fast as we can. Right?'

He stared at her, belligerence and suspicion warring on his face. But the bottom line was that he was a policeman. There were witnesses to this conversation, and no matter how much he might disagree with her he didn't want to lose his job.

He had to follow orders.

'Right,' he said, and he turned away from her. The branch he'd pushed aside was lowered carefully so it didn't hit her.

But his hand went again to his gun.

Sarah hesitated. She turned and found Alistair watching her, and by the look in his eyes she could see he was as worried as she was.

By mutual consent they fell back from Barry—just a little.

'Don't worry too much,' Alistair murmured, so low Barry couldn't hear. He motioned to the two women bushwalkers who were striding ahead in the manner of people who could go even faster than Flotsam. 'Daphne and Susan are two really sensible women. I've primed them.'

'You've primed them?'

'When we leave today they'll stay around, and when Jack comes out he'll join them. I've asked them to stick close to Barry. We both know he's a loose cannon, but he's not a crazy loose cannon. He'll stick to the law—especially if he has witnesses. I've organised that he always has witnesses.'

'Thank you.' Sarah took a deep breath. This man was good. He knew his people.

Maybe that was what being a country doctor was all about.

She thought back to the things she remembered Grant saying about him—'My brother, who intends to spend his life treating bunions and coughs and colds and all the imaginary ills of a pack of hayseeds.'

Grant had been wrong. This man was much more than that.

Alistair…the dull twin? She didn't think so.

She'd never thought so. And that was the trouble.

They hiked the rest of the way in uneasy silence, which suited Sarah perfectly. Barry had stopped his condescending slowness and now she was having trouble keeping up, but there was no way she was asking him to slow down on her behalf. She concentrated on her breathing and concentrated on her footing, and when she finally stumbled out onto the little beach where the plane lay Alistair touched her arm and smiled.

'Well done,' he said in an undervoice.

He didn't like her, she thought, but apparently he'd decided to put aside their antagonism in the face of a mutual enemy. She could cope with that. She could almost be grateful for it. She'd worked with difficult cops before, but never when the officer causing difficulties was the sole representative of the force. She gave Alistair an uneasy smile in response and the look on his face said he understood exactly.

His expression unnerved her. It was almost as if he had the

capacity to read her mind, and she found—increasingly—that it was a really disturbing sensation.

The job. Concentrate on the job.

The plane had crashed into the rockface but there was minimal damage. Blocking out everyone else, Sarah circled the tiny aeroplane until she was sure she understood what had happened. There should be flight investigators here, she thought—they'd come, but this was such a remote area the initial assessment had to be up to her.

What had happened seemed obvious. There were deep wheel marks gouged into the beach from the high tide mark. The pilot had intended to land. He'd been aware enough to get the plane down at the point where he'd had maximum run, and given luck he could have made it. He almost had.

While the others watched on—Barry with a look of truculence on his big face and the others expressionless—Sarah climbed into the cockpit. She stared around her. Things here were almost intact. Only the windscreen had been smashed. She could see how the pilot had sustained an injury to his face. She stared around, wanting more, but there was nothing else. A pile of girlie magazines had obviously been lying on the passenger seat. They'd slid off on impact, though a few had caught in the seat belt. That was all. There was no blood, apart from a slight smear on one of the magazines. No vomit. Nothing to suggest human distress of any kind.

Alistair was right behind her. Just outside the aeroplane. Waiting.

'The heroin hit must have been so fast,' she murmured, carefully collecting the magazine with the blood sample and slipping it into a plastic keeper. 'I'm wondering now whether the condom did burst in mid-air. It seems more likely that the build-up of material in his gut made him feel so ill that he had to land. He did have a real chance of getting down here. But as the plane hit the rockface the pressure of the seat belt would have burst the condom.' She frowned and looked around her once more. 'Either way, death would have been fast.'

'But not for the passengers,' Alistair said grimly, standing aside to let her climb from the cockpit and move to the cargo area.

She glanced at the ground—at the mass of footmarks. 'Site preservation?'

'There were people here before me,' Barry said a trifle belligerently. 'They hauled open the back doors.'

'The doors were all closed?'

'I think so.'

'Can you check? And see if anyone noticed whether there were any footmarks around the plane?' It would have been so easy if she'd been on hand straight away, she thought ruefully. All it would have needed was a look to see if there were footprints leading away from the plane, and they would have been easy to decipher in such soft sand. But to come in thirty-six hours after the event…

'Barry was the only one to go into the rear of the plane,' Alistair told her. 'After he saw the empty gun holster he had to, to see if there was a gun. I arrived about ten minutes after the first group—we sent the fastest walkers first—but already the scene was compromised.'

'You noticed?'

'I noticed that the scene was compromised. There were footprints everywhere. But no one but Barry went into the cargo area. It's too unpleasant.'

He was right there. Alistair hauled open the door into the back of the plane and she only needed a glance to know there'd been real human suffering here.

Someone had been ill. She could smell the vomit. And the blood.

'Major blood vessel,' she said softly. 'And the vomit… Airsick, maybe?'

'It looks like it,' Alistair told her.

'Mmm.' She stood at the entrance, taking careful note.

Heaving her backpack from her shoulders, she retrieved a flashlight, then shone it carefully, meticulously, around every section of the cabin.

'Someone lay there and bled,' she said, staring down at a dark, pooled stain. 'Why?' Then her eyebrows furrowed. 'Let's assume they were sitting down against the sides as they flew. People do. It gives them better balance. They usually don't sit in the middle of the aircraft. This is a small area, but assuming we don't have many people they'll have been sitting leaning against the sides. It fits with where the vomit is. As the plane came in to land they wouldn't have got to their feet. Maybe they'd have known enough to go into brace position. So what have we got that could have cut them? Caused this amount of damage?'

'They could have had a bloody nose like our pilot.'

'Too much blood. This is a major blood vessel. Our AB passenger hit himself on something sharp. Like…' She stared around some more and her eyes rested on a metal box. The thing looked as if it had been used as some sort of suitcase, but it was open and its edges were raw metal. Sarah leaned forward and ran her flashlight around the rim. And winced at what she saw. A tiny fragment of ripped cloth, what looked like skin and a dark smear of blood.

'I'm guessing here's our culprit. We have our passengers in brace position, or similar, but with nothing to hold on to as our plane crashed. They're feeling bad. These things are appalling to fly in even when they've got seats. So they come in to crash land. We have this thing free to fly around at will. My guess is that it's hit legs. More than one leg. Or a hip maybe. Whatever. Can we bag the whole thing and bring it back for examination?' Her flashlight kept searching.

'So we're looking for bodies?' Alistair asked.

'Maybe not.' Her flashlight was carefully inspecting the floor of the cabin. 'Where was the tarpaulin—does anyone know? Barry?'

The policeman came up behind them and stared in at the

mess over her shoulder, reluctantly co-operative. 'The tarp was over in the far corner.'

'Not near the door?'

'No.'

She nodded. 'So there's been no major bleeding near the door. If our man was bleeding to death and intent on getting out of the plane there'll have been a trail of blood leading out the door. The area around the door is almost clean.' She cocked her head to one side. 'What do you reckon was in that metal case?'

'Drugs,' the policeman said promptly, but Sarah shook her head.

'I doubt it.' She ran her flashlight over it once more. 'It looks to me like it's been used as a suitcase. My grandmother had one just like it. They're cheap and nasty—this one hasn't got a lock. It'll have been thrown open as the plane hit and the contents strewn everywhere. And what's in suitcases—usually—is clothes.'

'So?' said Barry, and there was no mistaking the note of belligerence in his voice. He obviously didn't hold with lady doctors telling him stuff he could well work out himself.

'So the clothes may well have been used to pad and bind wounds. To provide pressure. You say it took half an hour to get to the wreck? That's time for someone who knew what they were doing to fashion pressure pads and tie them in place, staunch the bleeding as best they could and then get the heck out of here. That's the only scenario I can think of that fits.'

'Which explains the empty case,' Alistair said thoughtfully, and she nodded.

'Then they're still alive.' Barry turned and stared up at the surrounding hills.

'But without drugs,' Sarah told him.

'Maybe.'

'And there's no signs of weapons,' Alistair added. 'I'd be happier if you put that damned pistol aside, Barry.'

'There was a gun. If they're drug-dealers…'

'Then they're drug-dealers who are in deep trouble,' Sarah snapped. She was starting to feel hugely uneasy about this man. Uneasy enough to radio headquarters and voice her concerns? Maybe. Or maybe she needed to, but not now. She'd wait until she got back to Dolphin Cove, she decided. The sooner they had another member of the police force here the better, no matter how many Heads of Commonwealth meetings there were. 'With this amount of bleeding, someone is near death,' she told him. 'We may well have someone in a coma on our hands. This is major injury, Barry.'

He shrugged. Clearly the idea of a few drug runners dying on his patch didn't unduly worry him.

'So how many?' he demanded.

'At least two.' Sarah played the flashlight over the floor of the cabin once more. And faltered. Her beam raked the floor again, and once again it stopped. 'Oh, no…'

'What?' Alistair was following her beam but not seeing.

'Barry, are you sure you're the only person who's been in here?' she demanded, and the policeman nodded.

'I'm sure.'

'No children came with you in the initial rescue team?'

'No.'

'I might be wrong, but there… Is it a child's footprint?' she whispered. 'See those smudges? It seems everyone has crawled out, leaving no identifying trace, and most footprints have been overlaid by Barry's. But there, against the wall…' She took a deep breath and refocussed. 'Can you hold my hand, Alistair? Support me while I lean in? I don't want to compromise this further.'

She climbed up into the cabin, stood just inside the doorway but didn't enter, reluctant to disturb the scene more than it had been already. But balancing just within, leaning inward and letting Alistair take all her weight, she could reach right into the cabin without disturbing the blood or the pattern of the smudged knee and footmarks.

She leaned until she was right over the place where she'd directed the torch. For a long moment she stared down, and the look on her face was grim as death.

'What is it?' Alistair said gently, and she knew he'd seen from her expression how deeply disturbed she was.

'It's definitely a child's,' she whispered. She was following the outlines with her torch, but the more she looked at it the more she knew she was right. 'It's the outline of a sandal, or something similar, and it's tiny. By the look of it we're looking at the print of a four or five-year-old.'

It changed things. Maybe it shouldn't, but it did. There was a deathly silence while they all took in this new piece of horror.

Finally Alistair eased her out. Sarah jumped down onto the soft sand and pushed her curls out of her eyes with an expression of intense weariness.

'I can't tell what's happened,' she said. 'I don't have the skills. But there are people who do. Footprints can give us age and weight, maybe even things like country of origin if the footwear is specific enough, but there'll be more evidence than footprints. DNA can be isolated for everyone who was on this plane. Meanwhile I don't know who they are or what they've done but I want them found. Barry, you might be right that they're hiding, but no matter what you think about their motives this fact is absolute: we have a child, probably badly injured, who for whatever reason is somewhere in the hills around here. I don't care what the security arrangements are for the Heads of Commonwealth. I'll ask for experts. I want this place analysed by the best forensic team we have and I want it done now. Or sooner!'

CHAPTER FOUR

SARAH made a careful inspection of the site, but there was nothing else it could tell her. She roped off the plane so no one else could go near, but she knew it was futile. 'It's like shutting the gate after the horse has bolted, but it's all I can do. I want technicians up here to take fingerprints. Anything. There's been so much messed up already...'

'I'm sorry,' Alistair said ruefully as they left the beach.

There was no point in their staying. Jack, the capable mechanic Alistair had spoken of, had arrived. He was primed to stay close to Barry. Alistair needed to be back at the hospital and Sarah needed to set wheels in motion—wheels that required a phone and a lot of explanation.

'To be honest, I wasn't thinking about compromising the scene,' Alistair told her. 'I had a dead pilot on my hands, and almost the moment I saw him there were people demanding I get back to town fast to cope with the suspected coronary. I thought...'

'You thought Barry might be depended on to preserve the site?'

'Yes.'

She considered. 'So, when he said there were others at the plane before him who messed with the footprints...'

'There weren't. He went out with the first group. I was following soon after, but Barry would have been first on the scene.'

'So he just didn't notice whether there were prints leading out of the plane before everyone else had stomped all over them.' She sighed. 'The man's a liar as well as a fool.'

'His mind's not exactly on the job. He doesn't want to be here.'

'The easiest way for him to get out is to learn to be a decent cop,' she said ruefully. 'What are the authorities about, sending someone like this to be a sole policeman in this remote place? Professionals without back-up have to be the best.'

'That's not something Grant would have said.'

She cast him a look that was disturbed. Professionals without back-up having to be the best? Alistair was right. Grant would never have conceded that. Even if it meant criticising his brother.

Grant had done nothing but look down with disparagement on his twin, Sarah thought. How much had that hurt?

'We were very young,' she said softly.

He said nothing.

They walked on. She had to concentrate. The path was really rough. But it was easier returning than going. Alistair was walking behind her but he was moving branches aside, holding them. Making the way easier for her.

Why was he suddenly being nice?

She and Grant…they'd been so conceited. At first she'd even gone along with Grant's disparagement of his family. Sure, she hadn't disparaged them herself, but she'd laughed at Grant's hayseed jokes.

Until she'd spent time with them.

Until she'd discovered what Alistair was really like.

'What do we do now?' Alistair asked, and she hauled herself back to the job at hand.

'Worry,' she said, trying to keep it light. 'It's what I'm principally good at.'

'Yet you decided not to stay at the plane with Barry?'

'I don't think they'll find them.'

'Why not?'

She hesitated. Why not? Gut instinct? No. Something more.

'They're running,' she said. 'There are at least two blood groups there, which means at least two people. But there's a child. I'm going to be really presumptuous here and assume if one's a child then there'll be parents. Why on earth would parents take an injured child and hide?'

'Maybe the child's hiding himself? Maybe the pilot was the kid's father?'

'He didn't look like a father.' She gave a rueful grin. 'I know. There's presumption again. But the passenger seat in the cockpit wasn't used.'

'How do you know?'

'There are magazines, not only on the floor but caught in the seat belt. No one was in that seat when the plane crashed. That little plane is designed to carry a pilot, one passenger and cargo. At low altitudes. The hold isn't pressurised. The cargo area is bare metal and there are no seats. It'll have been truly horrible to travel in. No wonder the passengers were ill. If the child was the pilot's son or daughter…'

'He'd have given the kid the passenger seat.' Alistair nodded. 'Yeah. I see that.'

'Or if anyone in the back was a friend he'd have had that seat. It's a Rolls-Royce ride compared to the one they got. Yet the magazines got the ride and no one else. It screams to me that our pilot was transporting people for money. That plane won't be licensed to carry any more passengers than one. The guy's an idiot. He's importing heroin in his stomach. He's transporting passengers. In these conditions there's no way these are pleasure flights. I'm guessing these passengers are in some sort of trouble. Major trouble.'

'Like what?'

'Who knows? Given that they've run, I'd guess there might well be criminal convictions. Barry might be right. I need to make a few phone calls—get enquiries underway. But as there's a child involved…' Her voice died.

'What?'

'I'm thinking that because of how far north you are,' she said slowly, 'and because of the fact that the plane flew north from Cairns, maybe landed and then headed west to this side of Cape York, maybe what we have here is a case of people-smuggling.'

'Illegal immigrants?'

'It makes more sense than anything else I can think of. Maybe they've been landed on the coast somewhere on the eastern side of Cape York by a charter boat, with the arrangement that our pilot will pick them up and take them somewhere they can be processed with false passports and the like. Somewhere really remote. Somewhere near here. How much fuel did the plane have left?'

'The mail run pilot said there was only enough for another half-hour in the air.'

'But most pilots verge on the safe side of caution,' she said, thinking out loud. 'Half an hour… You know, if I was a pilot in such rough country as this I'd leave plenty of margin for error. Say even twenty minutes' flight time. If there are cattle over the airstrip and they have to be cleared…well, anything could happen to delay landing. He's not coming to some place where a clear run can be guaranteed.'

'So what are you saying?'

'That we need to look at places close to here. Really close. Is there somewhere I can get a list of property owners?'

'Why?'

'I'm thinking…' She frowned. 'I'm thinking people who are involved in something as major as people-smuggling don't usually have clean criminal records. I know it's a longshot, but if you had a list of outlying property owners, or people who are renting or leasing, I could get a fast police check. Just to see if anything comes up.'

She trudged on. Alistair walked silently behind. She was conscious that his eyes were on her. She was being appraised. And found wanting?

Maybe not.

'I can help with that,' he said at last. 'I know that there are ethical issues involved, but as we're talking about people's lives, I think I can square it with my conscience. We don't have a pharmacy in Dolphin Cove. Pharmacy supplies are issued through the hospital. Through me. That means everyone who uses this town as a shopping base is registered here. I have a list of everyone who's had so much as a tetanus shot in the last twelve months. More, we register our users on our computer as local or remote. If they're remote we can issue people double or more supplies of prescription medication so they don't need to make the trip into town so often. I can run you off an alphabetical list of all adults categorised as remote in the region. Will that do?'

'Just like that?' she said, startled, and he smiled.

'Just like that. If you're sure…'

'I'm not sure,' she admitted. 'I'm not sure in the least. But it makes sense. Our pilot's just been to Thailand, so he may well have been contracted there to do the pick-ups once our visitors reached Australia. While he was in Thailand they must have been already on their way by boat. They must have come by boat. Bringing people in illegally by plane is almost impossible—our border defence will pick them up. But landing people by boat on a remote beach is easier. Internal flights aren't monitored, so maybe they'll be put off the boat somewhere north of Cairns. Meanwhile our pilot comes home to Australia to pick them up. He flies as a normal passenger on a commercial airline, but on the way he decides to make a profit on the side. He swallows the condoms. Once in Australia he hires his small plane, flies north to collect his passengers, brings them almost to their destination—and then he dies. Which means out there in the bush we have a group of terrified illegal immigrants, at least one of whom is a child. They won't come near any searchers. They'll have invested too much in getting to this country. And they won't know how savage this country can be.'

'You're basing a lot on supposition.'

'I am,' she agreed. 'If there'd been any major crime in the last few days and we had fugitives on the run I'd say that'd be a better explanation. But there's been nothing. This is the only scenario that fits with him flying north of Cairns before he came here.'

'If you're right,' Alistair said slowly, 'they'll know nothing. There's crocodiles in the freshwater streams and in the mangrove swamps. There are snakes—'

'And there's infection.' Sarah bit her lip and quickened her pace. 'We need to move fast. I don't see Barry as having the push to get people up here to help, but I'll sure as heck try. You're going back to town to turn into being the Dolphin Cove doctor for the day. I'm going back to turn into a force to be reckoned with. I'll have a major search and rescue unit up here, forensic scientists—the lot.'

'But if they still hide…'

'They'll come out,' Sarah said. 'They must. Please.'

They split when they reached the town. The tension between them had dissipated in the face of urgent professional need.

Alistair made arrangements for Sarah to have use of phones, faxes and radio; he helped her e-mail his list of the remote population to headquarters, so it could be matched against criminal files; he organised the mail run to come earlier—Sarah wanted samples to be taken fast to Cairns for urgent analysis, as DNA matching could give her more information—and then he left her to it.

Sarah—with Flotsam settled happily at her feet—sat on the phone for an hour. And another hour. Finally she rose and ran a hand wearily through her hair. She'd done all she could. Nothing was possible today. It would take a day to get all the resources she needed up here. It would take another few hours to do the cross-matching with population and criminal files. But at least things were in train.

But she was so frustrated.

What else could she do?

She walked out onto the veranda and stood looking up into the hills. If she was right, somewhere out there was a group of desperately injured, desperately frightened people. How on earth could she make them ask for help?

Barry wouldn't find them. They wouldn't let him.

She was going nuts. There had to be something she could do.

Walk the dog? Swim?

A swim sounded good, but she wasn't too sure about the beach. It looked deserted, and in her experience deserted beaches were usually deserted for a reason. It was May—too late for the worst of the nasties inhabiting tropical waters. She knew enough about box jellyfish and the like to afford them the respect they were due. She'd have to ask someone before she tried swimming.

She'd just wander over to the hospital.

She showered and changed—made the transformation from scratched and filthy bushwalker into something that might approximate a doctor, donning a fresh skirt, blouse and sandals—and made her way around to the hospital entrance.

She walked in and stopped in astonishment. There were maybe twenty people lined up on seats around the waiting area.

Good grief!

Claire was bustling past, carrying a specimen jar, and Sarah stopped her. 'What's going on? Trouble?'

Claire shook her head. 'Nope. Normal. Doc's been out of town all morning, and he's been called out again now to a place out of town—someone's rolled a tractor—and the fleet's in.'

'The fleet's in?'

'The weather's blowing a south-westerly,' Claire explained, 'That means all the fishing boats have headed back to town. Most of these guys spend three or four weeks at sea at a time and they come up with all sorts of nasties. Tropical waters. Heat. A scratch becomes septic. And they spend their spare time on board dreaming up symptoms. Not only that, but while the weather's bad these guys have all the time in the world to sit round here waiting for a consultation. If I tell them to come back in the morning I'll be wasting my breath. Alistair will have his hands full until midnight.'

Sarah stared round at the waiting room, stunned. And guilty. Alistair had taken time out he could ill afford this morning, and she knew half the reason he'd come was that he was concerned about Barry's behaviour. Which rightly was Sarah's responsibility.

She remembered the way he'd cleared the path for her on the way back and how he'd held her as she'd leaned into the plane. He'd made her work easier. Maybe she could do the same. She was a trained doctor, after all.

'Can I help?' she said—tentatively—and Claire grinned as if Sarah had just walked straight into a baited trap.

'You surely can. I thought you'd never ask. Can you treat a septic finger?'

'I really enjoy a good septic finger,' Sarah told her, discovering she was grinning in response. The nurse's cheerful good humour was infectious. 'A nice little bit of ooze—it's principally why I became a doctor.'

Claire's smile broadened. 'And then you became a forensic pathologist—that'd give you more ooze that even I want to think about.'

They were both smiling now. Claire was a woman in her early thirties—maybe a little older than Sarah, but not much. She was a squat little woman who looked competent and funny and…nice. She could be a friend, Sarah thought, and then she thought suddenly and irrationally that friendship was something she should work on. It was something that was lacking in her life. She didn't let people close. Not since Grant…

No. Not since Grant. So maybe friendship wasn't a good idea. She needed to move on.

'Show me a room with equipment and a prescription pad,' she said, breaking the moment with resolution. 'Ooze, eh? Let me at them.'

'Okay.' Claire turned Sarah round so she was facing twenty fishermen. 'Right, you guys, here's your new lady doctor. Sarah's not only competent but she's also a pathologist. That means she knows how to cut up bodies. So no one had better give her any cheek. Sarah, don't take anything from any one of them—if they step one inch out of line offer them a place on your mortuary slab. Let's go.'

She worked solidly for three hours. Claire ushered patients in one after the other, and, to her astonishment, Sarah found she was enjoying herself immensely.

This was real medicine. It was medicine she hadn't practised for five years, and even then she'd started her initial training as a paediatrician in a city hospital. Paediatrics wasn't this sort of medicine.

The fishing crews were rough, tough, but underneath as worried as mothers with newborns about their myriad ills. Most of them had been at sea for weeks, and in those circumstances—three weeks of thinking of nothing but sea and fish—minor complaints had a habit of growing in the mind if not in reality. A freckle on a forearm became a melanoma. A little deafness in one ear became a tumour. Sarah found most of her time was spent in reassurance. And apart from that, there were the festering sores that had been neglected for too long…

She worked through, being given an inquisition by each patient.

After Claire's good-natured injunction to behave with respect, they treated her with caution—but also with immense curiosity. 'How can you possibly be a forensic pathologist? We've seen what they do on telly. Why would anyone as pretty as you want to do that stuff?'

This community was heavily male-oriented. Single women were scarce as hen's teeth, and she was propositioned by at least five fishermen. She ended up chuckling as she saw out the last fisherman, listening to his impassioned plea to go out with him that night as she tried to close the door behind him.

'Yeah, I know we haven't got any restaurants, but I know this great secluded little cove, and I'll bring lobster and as much beer as we can drink.'

She grinned at him and declined, and was still laughing when she turned to find Alistair watching her, an expression of stunned incredulity on his face.

'What on earth do you think you're doing?'

She didn't stop smiling. 'I suspect I'm protecting my virtue. If he hasn't got more than lobster and beer on his mind then I'm a monkey's uncle.'

'I mean—' he wasn't smiling '—seeing my patients.'

'It's unethical, isn't it?' she agreed. 'But Claire said you were snowed under. You needn't worry. The people I saw only had minor worries. Anything that I was the least concerned about I saved for you, or told them to come back in the morning for a repeat consultation with a real doctor. For instance you.'

'Thank you very much,' he said dryly, and her smile faded.

'Well, I think you *should* say thank you,' she retorted. 'I've saved you three hours' work.'

'While you should be out solving crime?'

'As far as I know there's no crime to solve. There are missing people I'm doing my best for, but there's not a lot I can do but wait.'

'And do nothing?'

'And do your work.' Her anger was building.

'I didn't ask you—'

'I offered. I'm not incompetent, Alistair. I'm not sure why you came with me this morning, but—'

'I'm not suggesting you're incompetent, either.'

'Then let's leave it,' she snapped. 'We're both competent doctors. You help me and I'll help you. That's fair.'

'I don't need help.'

'No? You could be just starting clinic now and coping with

everything else all on your own. If I was anyone else but me would you be so ungracious?'

He hesitated. Then met her gaze square-on. 'No,' he admitted.

'Then why—'

'There's too much history, Sarah. What you did…'

She closed her eyes. What she did… It hung over her like a great black fog. An admission of guilt she could never escape.

When she opened her eyes Alistair's expression had changed. 'Sarah…' His brows had snapped down as if he was suddenly uncertain. That was a change, she thought bleakly. The black cap of judgement had been replaced by something that had just the faintest shade of grey about it.

It didn't matter. It couldn't matter. What this man thought of her was totally immaterial.

'I need to go through my notes with you,' she told him.

'Why?'

'If there's something you disagree with then you can dash out and change the medication before I kill someone else.'

Kill someone else. It was a bleak and harsh statement and it hung. Dreadful.

And Alistair's face changed yet again. Acknowledging the pain she had no hope of disguising.

'You've lived with the guilt of Grant's death for six years,' he said softly, and she didn't say anything at all. Nothing. There was nothing to say.

If she'd wanted to say something then the time to do that had been six years ago, she acknowledged bleakly. Not now. Not now, when it was far, far too late to change a thing.

'Sarah, I—'

'Leave it,' she said, more roughly than she'd intended. 'Alistair, we agreed to shelve it. We need to work together for the next couple of days, until we sort this out, and then we can move on. We don't have to see each other again after this. But for now we need to be civil. The way I see it, the only way we can do that is if we avoid the subject completely.'

'There are unresolved issues—'

'Then they're staying unresolved.'

'Right.' There was a moment's silence while each of them regrouped. Figured out where to go from here. Finally...

'You're telling me you've done all my work?' Alistair said cautiously, and Sarah practically groaned in relief. They were back to being medical colleagues. It was a relationship she could cope with. She couldn't cope with anything more.

He even sounded as if he intended to be nice again.

Well, two could go down that path.

'Yep.' She even managed a smile. 'Plus your ward round. Mr Carter's heart is behaving itself. Don dropped in and had his shoulder checked—he's doing nicely. It looks to me as if it's only the result of his major fall—I doubt it'll end up being a chronic problem. How's your guy under the tractor?'

'He's okay. He was pushed into soft dirt. He had breathing trouble until we got the thing off him, but once the pressure was off he recovered almost immediately. He has two broken ribs. I've put him into hospital for observation but he should be fine.'

'Lucky.'

'He is.' Alistair's gaze was thoughtful. His eyes were appraising her. 'Are you tired?'

'Why should I be tired?' She was ready to spring onto the defensive.

But he was still in nice mode. 'You've had a long day.'

She glanced at her watch. 'It's only six.'

'And you've just knocked back a dinner invitation.'

'So I did,' she said, finally relaxing a little. Alistair seemed to have moved on—away from the hurtfulness of a past that was almost unbearable—and if he was prepared to do that then she was only too glad to follow. 'I liked the idea of beach and lobster, but the beer and seduction bit was maybe a spot over the top.'

'So if I said lobster and beach, with no seduction included…?'

'Anyone who says lobster and beach has my complete compliance,' she told him. 'Lobster, beach. Two of my very favourite things. In fact, if I hadn't been so scared of scary things I'd be on the beach right now.'

'Scary things?'

'The beach was deserted this afternoon,' she told him. 'It looked gorgeous, but with no lifesaver in sight and no one in the water I assumed there must be at least half a dozen lethal-type stingers like box jellyfish lurking out there.'

'They don't come in at this time of the year.'

'Then why isn't the town swimming?'

'It's a normal school day,' he told her. 'The townspeople are working. The fishermen are in port, but the last thing they want when they're in port is any more sea. And anyone who has any free time is out searching. Not wasting time swimming.'

'Well,' she said, meeting his gaze square-on, 'that's put me in my place properly, hasn't it?' She gave him a half-hearted smile. 'You're very good at it.'

'I don't have a clue what your place is.'

Silence. Neither knew where to take it from there. But…he had said lobster and beach…

'Cooked lobster?' she queried, and the tension eased off again as he smiled.

'Yep. One of the fishermen who's just come in cooked up a batch this afternoon. He always keeps me some. It saves me from Mrs Granson's interminable casseroles for a day or so.'

'You know,' she said thoughtfully, 'you could always learn to cook.'

'I need a wife,' he said—and the twinkle was suddenly back behind his eyes again. She liked it, she thought. More. She loved it. Well, she must. Grant had had just that same twinkle.

No. It was different. Grant's twinkle had led to nothing but disaster. Alistair's twinkle promised teasing and lobster and a swim. Nothing more.

'I need a wife, too,' she said, responding to his smile. 'Anything to save me from a casserole like last night's. But if it's only you that's offering…well, Dr Benn, I accept you and your lobster as a wife substitute.'

'Thanks very much,' he said faintly, and she grinned.

'Any time. Lobster, eh? Is it a large lobster?'

'Maybe it can even be stretched to two lobsters.'

'You're definitely wife material,' she told him. 'Lead on.'

The beach was magic.

The tide here was huge, which meant that at low tide there was almost three hundred yards of golden sand. The tide was coming in now, though, which meant it took only fifty or sixty yards to reach the water. Sarah walked onto the sand, looked out at the waves lapping the shore and simply shed her clothes as a butterfly shed its cocoon. Her bikini was underneath, but, watching her, Alistair thought she was almost unaware of it.

She was certainly unaware of him. She'd walked down here by his side, with Flotsam bouncing next to her. Her face had been tilted to the sun and she'd seemed almost oblivious to his presence.

Which was a huge difference for him.

The Benn twins had been born good-looking. There had never been a dearth of women in their lives, and Grant had moved from one fabulous-looking woman to the next. Alistair had always been more selective, and so far there'd never been a woman who'd attracted him enough to make him want to commit to marriage, but he had always been aware that women were attracted to him.

Maybe that was why Grant had been infatuated with Sarah, he thought. Sure, she was gorgeous—and, sure, her father was so rich he could afford to give his daughter anything, which would have appealed to Grant enormously—but there was something more. Grant had offered her marriage. He'd told

Alistair that this was the one and maybe Alistair could see why.

She might be rich, but she didn't flaunt it. She might be spoiled rotten by indulgent parents, but she was a hard-working doctor who pulled her weight and expected no concessions to her status.

And she hardly seemed aware of the fact that any man's hormones would start an immediate riot the minute she walked in the door.

He stood on the shoreline for a while, watching as Flotsam barked in hysteria and Sarah splashed the little dog and laughed at him until he gave up and started chasing gulls instead. Then she turned to face out to sea, seemed to gather herself, and dived under the first wave and started swimming strongly.

She swam the same way she approached life—with confidence and expertise. Her lithe body sliced effortlessly through the surf.

He watched.

Flotsam came haring up the beach, shaking water all over his legs, and he laughed and bent to pat the little dog.

'You think I should go in and join her?'

Of course he did. They both did.

But joining her would be a bit difficult. She was lapping the beach, swimming steadily up and down the limits of the little cove. Outer reefs protected this beach. The surf was mild and kind. You could swim for hours.

She could swim for hours.

'And what fun is that?' Alistair asked Flotsam. 'How do we distract her?'

Why would he want to distract her?

Impossible question to answer. All he knew was that he did want to do just that, and he had the means right in the picnic basket.

He lifted the cloth and removed a couple of bread rolls. 'They're not for you,' he told Flotsam. 'They're to make the lady play.'

He was standing in a washing machine.

Sarah turned for a repeat lap of the cove and her attention was caught. Alistair was standing waist-deep in the surf and the water around him was a white, churning, maelstrom of movement. Silver slivers were leaping around him—the whole sea looked alive to within twelve feet of the man.

Entranced, she found her feet and stared, breast-deep in the water and fifty feet from the action.

'You want to try?' he asked, and she hesitated.

'Try what?'

'Fish feeding.'

'You're kidding?' But as she watched he lifted his hand and scattered a fistful of crumbs around him. The water erupted. Slivers of silver fish leaped, contorting, brushing him, desperate to reach the crumbs.

'Like to try?' He held out a bread roll.

How was a girl to resist an invitation like that? She dived down and swam strongly underwater, opening her eyes as she neared him.

Fish. Everywhere were fish. Gorgeous silver arrows, long and thin and darting with magic speed... There must be hundreds of them.

She surfaced right by Alistair's legs and the fish didn't care at all. They were surfacing all around her, brushing her face, swimming through her hands.

She'd never seen anything like it. Entranced, she floated while all about her the fish leaped and tumbled and just...

Just were.

'It's a real-life spa,' she whispered, and Alistair grinned.

'Want to see me turn the power up?' He tossed another handful of crumbs and the water around them churned with the horsepower of a commercial washer. Sarah lay back, grinning like a fool. She'd come down to the beach determined to keep her distance, but who could keep their distance from an experience like this?

Not Sarah.

'This is magic,' she breathed as he handed over a bread roll and turned into a spectator himself. She crumbled the bread and lowered it into the water so it would just float away from her hand.

It didn't have a chance. The fish were actually lifting it from her fingers, darting away and then surging forward for more.

She was laughing out loud.

'What are they?'

'Mostly whiting. Though those guys there are banded grunters.'

'Banded who?'

'Banded grunters.' He grinned. 'You catch one and you'll see why they're called that. But you can't catch one here. The local fishermen have declared this area off-limits to preserve breeding grounds. So we have everything here. Even sea snakes.'

'Sea snakes?'

'Sea snakes. That's one winding through your legs right at this minute.'

'Right at this minute?' To say she froze would be an understatement. 'There's a snake winding through my legs...?'

'Look.'

'I'm carefully not looking,' she whispered.

'It wants some crumbs. Not you. Crumbs taste better.'

'Gee, thanks.'

'It's gone now.' He grinned at her still frozen expression and pointed to where a streak of silver-grey was breaking the surface as it snaked away. 'He's had his feed. He doesn't need a dessert of toes.'

She relaxed. Sort of. She tossed another lot of crumbs and relaxed some more. Sea snake or not, this was an experience that was almost unbelievable.

'People would pay a fortune for an experience like this,' she murmured, and Alistair smiled in agreement.

'They would. And so would those guys.'

'Who?' She looked up from her mass of writhing, tumbling fish and found he was pointing to the other side of the rocky outcrop protecting the little beach. A ring of rocks around the cove made it totally secluded. There was no fear of sharks coming in here. At high tide the rocks would be covered by about a foot of water, she thought, but now the ring of rocks was exposed. And outside it…

Fins. It was all she could do not to yelp. Rocks or not, there were fins, and her toes suddenly felt very vulnerable.

Sea snakes. Fins. A lesser woman might be clutching Alistair's neck right now, huddled into his arms.

Come to think of it…

No. Concentrate on fins.

'Sharks?' she quavered, and his smile widened.

'Look again.'

She did. The fins were cruising up and down on the other side of the rocks. Then whatever was under one of the fins seemed to take a chance. The creature surged forward, leaping into the air as if trying to see over the rock barrier. And Sarah gasped in sheer joy.

'Dolphins!'

'You can't imagine how frustrated they must feel,' Alistair told her. 'They're watching us feeding what they'd like as their dinner. The whiting and grunters come in here in schools and they're perfectly safe. The dolphins, however, have to live with frustration.'

'You tease them,' she said wonderingly, and he grinned.

'I do. They don't mind. There's heaps of fish on their side of the barrier.'

'Can we get closer?'

'I'd imagine with your swimming ability you'd be able to get as close as you like. And they'll be as interested in you as you are in them. I don't believe they've ever met a forensic pathologist before.'

'Don't tell them what I do,' she said urgently—half seriously. 'Let them think I'm a schoolteacher or something.' Then, before he could question her, she'd turned and dived through the small wavelets and was stroking firmly towards the rocks.

Alistair watched her for a moment—just watched her—and then followed.

CHAPTER FIVE

THE dolphins were the stuff of fantasy. Sarah sat on the rock ledge with water lapping over her toes and watched, seemingly entranced, while Alistair watched from behind.

What had that last comment meant? he wondered. Didn't she like being a forensic pathologist? Hadn't she been free to be whoever she wanted to be?

He knew so little about her, he realised. She'd been his brother's chosen wife and yet she was a total enigma.

Or maybe not completely. What did he know? Only what was written in the sort of glossy magazines Claire collected for his waiting room.

So he did know something. Sarah Rose was the daughter of a media magnate and one of his numerous wives. Alistair knew nothing of her mother—she seemed to have faded into insignificance since her brief marriage—but Sarah had been raised by her famous father in a glare of publicity, where very public marriages, very public divorces and far, far too much money were the order of the day. She had four half-sisters, all much older than Sarah and all of whom had gone on to be society wives of wealthy men. Sarah, though, had surprised the jet set by quietly going off to medical school. She'd surprised them even more by doing well.

Alistair remembered the first phone call he'd had from Grant. 'Hey, I've got a date with Sarah Rose. *The* Sarah Rose. How cool is that? Wish me luck, twin. Money, looks, class and brains—the girl has everything.'

Maybe she did have everything, but now… What did she have now? Shadows, he thought. He watched her as she watched the dolphins, hugging her knees and smiling that enigmatic little smile that told him of inner pleasure. Where was her jet-setting past in all this?

Would she ever have been happy with Grant?

Grant would have been happy with her, he thought bleakly. She was everything Grant had ever wanted in a woman.

She was everything *he* ever wanted in a woman.

No. She wasn't. That was a crazy thing to think. There were parts of her hidden right now. She might be sitting on her rock as if she desired nothing more in the world than to wiggle her toes in the water and watch dolphins at play, but behind her was money and corruption and a sleaziness that he couldn't begin to comprehend. She'd been drugged when she drove the car that killed Grant.

She was all things to all people, he thought savagely. She came here and she acted as a competent doctor—a competent pathologist—and indeed she was. But put her back in the city and she'd fit right back into her social milieu and heaven help any poor sod that got in her way.

She wanted to be a schoolteacher instead of a forensic pathologist? An ordinary person? That was a joke. She just wanted to play at life, as she always had.

'Aren't you coming?' She was turning to him, laughing with the delight of the moment.

'I'll watch from here,' he told her, and watched the shadows shutter down on her face. It had been a verbal slap and she'd felt it.

Damn, he felt a rat. For no good reason. What was he supposed to do—court her?

Her pleasure had faded but she was still looking determinedly bright. 'Can I swim out to them?'

That was easier. 'Of course you can swim out to them.'

'Won't there be sharks?'

'Sharks don't like dolphins. You don't need to worry.'

'How perfect.' She stood, took a deep breath, and hesitated just for a moment before she dived in.

And he had to agree. She was perfect.

Or not completely perfect. He frowned—just a little—noticing something for the first time. There was a long, jagged scar running the length of her left thigh. On anyone less lovely than Sarah it might not be noticed, but on Sarah…

No. The scar would be noticed anyway. It must have been caused by a major trauma.

Had that happened in the car accident when Grant had been killed? He frowned again, trying to remember. He'd hardly enquired as to the extent of Sarah's injuries.

There'd been no need. It had seemed such a minor accident. He remembered the call—Grant ringing to tell him about it.

'Sarah's smashed my car,' Grant had told him. 'Dratted women drivers. I should never have let her take the wheel in the first place. And it's a pain because I'd promised to come home and see the oldies this weekend for Dad's birthday. Tell them I can't come, will you?'

It had been yet another excuse for Grant not to visit their parents, Alistair had thought. It had sounded really minor, but he'd also known enough of Grant's lack of concern for others to enquire further.

'What sort of smash? Was anyone hurt?'

'Sarah's got a bit of concussion and minor lacerations,' Grant had told him. 'Nothing serious. Hell, she deserves something. She drove like a maniac on a road with ice on it, so maybe it'll teach her to slow down in the future. I've got a bit of a stiff neck but that's all.' He'd laughed down the phone, as he always had when trying to brush things aside. 'As far as I can tell the tree Sarah hit doesn't even need stress counselling. But my gorgeous car… The passenger side's crumpled all along the wheel base. It'll take weeks to repair. Tell Mum and Dad it'll be a month before I get home.'

'Did you get your neck X-rayed?' Alistair had asked—only because he was a doctor and it was an automatic reflex where head and neck injuries were concerned. But Grant had laughed again.

'Hey. I'm the older twin. I'm supposed to do the worrying. It was a slight bump that's not about to give me grief.'

So Alistair hadn't worried—until the next morning when Grant's cleaning lady had found him in bed. Dead. He'd refused advice to have his neck X-rayed—there'd been a party he was late for and he couldn't be bothered—and during the night an undisplaced fracture of the vertebrae had shifted.

Death would have been instantaneous. End of story.

And all Alistair's attention had had to be on his distraught parents. Alistair hadn't gone near Sarah. He'd read the police report, stating there were drugs present in Sarah's blood, and he'd been so angry he hadn't gone near.

But what had Grant meant when he'd said minor lacerations? He gazed across at her lovely tanned legs with their marring white streak and thought, This was never a minor laceration.

At the funeral Sarah had been on crutches.

So was he supposed to feel sorry for her?

No. He couldn't. But as her long, lithe body slipped seamlessly into the water and she started stroking out towards the dolphins he thought suddenly that he'd very much like it if he could.

He left her alone. It was the only thing to do.

Alistair swam by himself for a little, and then made his way up the beach to the picnic basket. Sarah joined him five minutes later, flinging herself down onto the sand and rolling like a sensual puppy in the sun-warmed sand. She rolled and rolled and then she pushed herself up and grinned.

'It stops sunburn,' she told him, correctly interpreting his look of astonishment. 'I coat myself like a rissole and, hey, cheap sun protection.'

'Have some lobster,' he said faintly, and she smiled and took a dollop of the lovely white flesh straight from the shell.

'Yum. Heaven.'

It was all he could do not to stare. She was growing lovelier and lovelier.

'Wine?'

She shook her head. 'Nope,' she said. 'I don't.'

'You don't drink?'

'No.'

'Not wine?'

'Not alcohol,' she told him. 'My mother had a problem. There's heaps of medical research saying alcoholism is a genetic trait. I figured early I could do without the risk.'

'You went out with Grant but you didn't drink?' More and more he was feeling stunned.

'That's right.'

'But you used other things to make up for it,' he said, and her hand stilled in the process of taking the lobster meat to her mouth.

There was a moment's silence while she appeared to consider how to answer him. And finally she forced her hand onward. Forcing herself to relax. Seemingly forcing herself not to slap him.

'This lobster isn't as good as I thought it would be,' she said. 'I think we should finish it fast and go home.'

She showered and went straight to her bedroom, and he didn't blame her. He'd messed it. He shouldn't be sorry, he decided—after all, her actions six years back were unforgivable and she should never be allowed to forget them—but all the same...

He showered himself, and did a ward round, and tried to do some paperwork, but all he could think of was the look of blind pain as he'd accused her.

But you used other things to make up for it.

It had been an appalling thing to say.

It was the truth. She'd killed his twin.

No. Grant had been in it up to his neck. The accident report had said that Grant had obviously been drinking. They hadn't breathalysed him because he hadn't been driving, but it had been clear. That was probably why he hadn't had the sense to agree to X-rays, and it was certainly why he'd been stupid enough to allow a clearly drug-influenced Sarah to take the wheel.

Could he ever stop thinking about it? He must. He had work to do.

He had a life to live.

The phone call came through at about nine-thirty and Alistair called Sarah out of her bedroom to take it. She'd obviously decided sleeping naked in this house was a bad idea. She emerged wearing pale pink pyjamas—cute ones—and fluffy slippers. Her pyjamas had clouds all over them, and her soft auburn hair swished against the silk of her pyjamas as she stalked past him to take the phone.

He was being sent to Coventry, he realised and thought suddenly that Sarah was really cute when she was angry.

She was also businesslike. She had a pad and pencil in her hand as she emerged. The call was from the crime squad in Sydney—the team who'd done the cross-matching of locals with criminal records for her. The call took a while, and her notes were extensive at the end of it.

Alistair was brushing the sand out of Flotsam's coat while she talked, trying not to listen. Trying not to think how cute she looked. She put down the phone and started back for her room.

'Can I help?' he said softly, and she hesitated. But he knew she needed help, regardless of the fact that neither of them wanted to be near each other.

'You have a list of locals with some sort of police record,' he told her. 'That's no use at all without local knowledge. I have a lot more of that than Barry does.'

She sighed and swung round to face him. Her gorgeous hair swished against the silk again. He shouldn't even be thinking how beautiful it was—but it was—and he was!

'I'm not supposed to show lists of criminal convictions to you. It's unethical.'

'You'd rather go through them with Barry?'

'No.'

'Well, then. What use is a list of possibilities without local knowledge? I know where they live, whether they're dead or not, whether there's anything to say they can't be involved.'

She hesitated.

'Go on,' he said, frustrated. 'You know you need to. If we get this over then we can go back to hating each other afterwards. Agreed?'

She glared—but she was obviously stuck. He had a point and she obviously knew it. 'Fine,' she said at last. 'Can we go through them now?'

'I'm ready when you are. Shall I make some tea?'

'I'll make my own tea,' she snapped. 'I'm here to work. Nothing else. Tonight was a big, big mistake. Work or nothing, Alistair. Right?'

'Right.'

So they sat and went through the list. One after the other. And somehow they kept their minds on the job at hand. Somehow.

Luckily there were things on the list that were really distracting.

'Hilda Biggins has a criminal record?' Alistair stared down at the list, astounded. 'She's the head of the Country Women's Association. I'd have sworn she's never had so much as a parking ticket in her life.'

'It says here she stole four bricks from a building site when she was a student,' Sarah told him. 'Thirty years ago. I bet she used them to make bookshelves or something really minor, and here it is, still showing up thirty years later. What a way to get a conviction. It's probably shocked her into leading a blameless life since.'

'I guess we can cross her off our list, then.'

'Unless she's been harbouring a secret resentment all these years,' Sarah said thoughtfully. 'Four bricks and she was caught. Resentment builds. She spends a life under cover, making pumpkin scones and running cake stalls, and then—wham—big-time crime. You haven't noticed her buying any dark sunglasses lately, have you?'

Alistair grinned. Sarah really was a chameleon, he thought. When she wasn't remembering the past she was just… enchanting. He could see how his twin had fallen so heavily for her.

He could see how he could fall just as heavily. How he already had…

No. He was trying really hard not to see any such thing.

'No sunglasses,' he managed, somehow managing to focus on Hilda. 'Actually, I think she's in Sydney at the moment, visiting a daughter who's just had a baby.'

'Aha! That'll be a ruse. She's probably recruiting hit-men as we speak.'

He choked at the thought of the buxom and matronly Hilda with dark glasses and hit-men. The tension eased and they worked their way through the list with the bitterness of the past somehow set aside.

It took a while.

'I'm really not supposed to be showing you this,' Sarah told him, growing more and more uncomfortable as Alistair looked at a more recent conviction for assault against the name of yet another pillar of the community. Alistair nodded with a certain amount of sympathy.

'I know you're not. And of course I won't use them. But Herbert Storridge…' He frowned. 'I've been a bit worried about Herbert's wife and kids, and this makes me even more worried. Amy Storridge has a haunted air, and last month one of the kids had a broken arm that didn't sound right. Herbert's a stalwart of the church, but he's never seemed…well, honest, if you like. Now here's a jail sentence for assault and it's only three years back. Just before he moved here. I might make enquiries. And keep an eye…'

'But he's not our problem,' Sarah said gently.

'He's my problem. Or at least his wife and kids are.' He

shook his head. 'It's neat for you, isn't it? Compartmentalise one problem, solve it or file it and then move on. Country medicine isn't like that.' Then, at her raised eyebrows, he grimaced, acknowledging priorities. 'But you're right. We need to focus.' He looked down again at the list. 'What about Howard Skinner?'

'Howard Skinner?'

'He's on your list.' Alistair thought about it. 'He's a possibility. He's come up with a conviction for fraud six years back. It must have been a fairly major fraud as he got two years' jail.'

'Where does he live?'

'That's just it,' Alistair said. 'He's overseer of a property about thirty miles from here. The place is owned by an international conglomerate that never goes near the place. Since the last drought they've hardly stocked it—it's been let go. It's my belief it'll soon be sold. But meanwhile Howard lives there alone.'

'It's a bit of an odd job,' Sarah said thoughtfully. 'How did he get it? Overseer to an outback cattle property when you've been a fraudster? I'd have thought they'd run a check for criminal convictions.'

'Overseeing derelict properties is a bit of a thankless task,' Alistair said. 'Sitting out in a dust bowl all by yourself, preventing squatters and vandals wrecking the place. Most owners have to take who they can get. It's hard enough to attract employees to the prosperous stations.'

'Do you know Howard?'

'I treat him for gout. He's a loner. Drinks a bit, but who can blame him?'

'Where does he get his supplies?'

'The local store, I imagine. He comes in once a fortnight or so.'

'Is the storekeeper a helpful type?'

Alistair grinned at that. 'That'll be Max Hogg. Max will be

so helpful you need to put aside the entire morning to be helped.'

'I'll wander into the store tomorrow,' Sarah said thoughtfully, staring down at the list.

'Why?'

'Because if Howard's involved in people-smuggling, he'll need more than one can of baked beans a day. He looks our most likely prospect. A guy on his own on a disused property. People could be taken there and given a crash course in assimilation. Fitted out with false documents and then taken on to cities or other rural communities. Maybe even bled into industries where cheap labour is short. It's a possibility.'

'It's a long shot.'

'It's better than doing nothing.' She looked up from the list and her green eyes flashed fire. 'You don't know how frustrating it is. Those people—if they're who I think they are, if my suppositions are correct—they're in a foreign land. They'll be scared stiff and they'll be wounded.'

'The searchers are doing the best they can.'

'They won't want to be found.' Sarah sighed and rose, stretching cat-like. 'I'm pooped. I need my bed. But tomorrow I'll talk to the store owner and then I'll pay a visit to your Howard. If I can organise transport.'

'You'll go out there alone?'

'Yeah. If I can borrow some transport. I'll figure out some pretext for dropping in.' She grinned. 'Guys are usually nice to me when I drop in.'

'I'll come with you,' he said, before he could stop himself, and her smile faded.

'Nope. That wouldn't be just a tourist being a nosy parker. It'd make him suspicious.'

'I don't know what you hope to achieve.'

'I don't either,' she agreed. 'But if I could find out who they are…if I could find out their nationality…I could get interpreters up here. I could get a paper drop in their own language, telling them that illegal arrival isn't a hanging offence and we'll look after them first and ask questions later. I could do… I don't know. Something.'

He stared at her and then rose slowly to his feet. 'You care, don't you?'

'Why ever would I not?'

He thought back to the Sarah he'd met six years ago. Not the Sarah whose first impression had been so wonderful, but the Sarah whose image he'd held in his head for six long years. A Sarah who took party drugs; who was rich and spoiled; who cared for nothing but herself.

Had she changed—or had she always been like this but he hadn't been able to see?

He was seeing now. He was staring at her as if he'd never seen her before. She was gazing up at him, her eyes questioning, and suddenly…suddenly—irrationally—crazily—she was just there—she was so close—she was so beautiful and he wanted to so much…

Stupidly, senselessly, and for no reason at all, he took her into his arms and kissed her.

What was it supposed to be? A kiss of what? A kiss of why? There was absolutely no logic behind this kiss—no reason at all that this couple were being hauled in together as if they were magnetised, magnet to metal, irresistible force meeting irresistible object.

Whatever the logic—or the lack of logic—what was between them now was unmistakable. It was a full-blown explosion. The moment Sarah's lips met Alistair's the whole world changed.

Or stopped.

What was happening here? This was crazy, Alistair thought as he felt passion surge between them. There'd been nothing but businesslike efficiency and a coldness caused by shadows that the past could never eradicate.

But now… Now he was holding her, kissing her, this slip of a girl with her wondrous green eyes, with her glorious hair, with her beautiful silk pyjamas…

He was kissing Sarah.

And there was the nub of it. She was Sarah. No more and no less. Sarah. She was kissing him back, he thought dazedly, and she was kissing him as he wanted to be kissed. Her lips were opening slightly under his mouth. Her body was yielding to his, her breasts moulding against his chest. Her arms were holding him as he was holding her.

She was on fire!

No. It was he who was on fire.

The heat of the moment was almost overpowering. His body felt as if it was melting inside, being consumed, transformed, changing to something he hardly recognised.

He wanted this woman and he wanted her with a force that was outside his imagining.

Sarah…

His hands were moving almost of their own volition. They were holding her waist, hauling her close. Closer. And, joyously, she was yielding. Yielding with such sweetness. Her lips were fastened on his. He could feel her tongue against his mouth. He could taste her…

Sarah. Her name was a prayer. A joyous refrain. A desperate, aching need.

What was happening? How had this started?

But he knew how it had started. He knew. It had started six long years ago, when he'd first stared down at her on the floor of the kids' ward and he'd fallen in love.

In love.

The words slammed into some dark recess of his brain, registered, shocked.

Love.

She was his twin's fiancée. She was Grant's love. She had nothing to do with him.

She was a part of him that had died along with Grant. A searing, aching pain that could never go away.

An impossibility.

And she felt it. He could sense the moment when she tensed

and moved back, just a fraction, so she could see his face. Her eyes resting on his were huge in the shadowed light cast by the table lamp. She looked ethereal. Not of this world.

She'd destroyed Grant, he thought desperately. She could well destroy him.

'What…what do you think you're doing?' she asked, in a voice that was distinctly tremulous, and he tried to collect himself. He tried to think.

Had he kissed her against her will? How had this craziness started?

He hardly knew. Somehow he dragged himself back. They stared at each other and his horror was reflected in Sarah's eyes. She was as appalled as he was, he thought. She hadn't wanted to kiss him.

But she had.

And he'd kissed her.

'It's hormones,' he managed, and his voice came out a sort of hoarse croak. 'I never meant…'

'Neither did I.'

'It's those pyjamas.'

'It's because you look like Grant.'

Yeah. There it was.

Grant.

He lay between them like a physical barrier that they could never overcome. Alistair's twin. The other half of his whole.

Sarah's fiancée.

'I need to go to bed,' she whispered, and he nodded.

'So do I.'

'Goodnight.' And she didn't wait for an answer. She turned and she fled.

CHAPTER SIX

WHAT followed was a really long night.

Sarah tossed and turned until dawn. Flotsam came and joined her in the bedroom for a while, and she was really grateful for the little dog's company. Then the dog padded off down the corridor and she heard the bedsprings creak in the other bedroom, Alistair's voice murmuring a greeting.

Flotsam was obviously going back and forth between the two of them.

An hour later Flotsam wuffled back. He snuggled in and Sarah thought, It's as if he wants us to be together. Man and woman with dog between.

Yeah. Great. Really ridiculous fantasy.

She desperately wanted to get up and make a cup of tea—anything to make the night go faster—but she was afraid that Alistair would have the same idea. She heard him rise a couple of times. The phone rang once—someone looking for advice on a child with croup. Through these thin walls she could hear everything. The child was obviously on an outstation a long way from town.

She listened to Alistair's patient, measured advice; she waited for him to hang up but then frowned to herself as he didn't. She realised he was waiting. He was holding onto the end of the line to see if his instructions were effective.

She imagined herself as the mother, on an outstation somewhere, maybe hundreds of miles from town. Croup was just plain scary. She'd be desperately worried as the child fought for breath. In the city there'd be a brief call for advice and then a trip into hospital or a call to the ambulance.

Here the mother was obviously too far away for those

things to happen. She had to cope herself—but Alistair was staying with her every step of the way.

Standing in the corridor in the middle of the night and just being with her.

There was intermittent conversation. The mother must be coming back and forth to the phone. Alistair stayed on the line for about half an hour, and by what he was saying Sarah could tell the breathing had finally eased.

She found herself relaxing. If she was alone with a sick child it'd be Alistair she'd want at the end of her phone, she realised.

He was so…good.

But so judgemental. What he thought of her…

She couldn't bear it.

She had to bear it. She'd made a choice six years ago and she had to live with it. For ever.

The phone call had been almost welcome. In the bedroom next door Alistair had quietly been going out of his mind. When Elaine Ferran had called about Lucy with croup it had been all he could do to stop himself offering to drive the eighty miles out to the property to cope with the croup himself.

Which would have been crazy. By the time he'd got there the croup would have been so bad Lucy's life would have been in danger or she'd have been better. Either way the obvious decision had been to treat her at the end of the telephone.

But Sarah was right through the wall. Her door was slightly ajar. Flotsam had wiggled past him in the hall and walked straight into Sarah's bedroom. Just like that. The dog would probably right now be jumping onto Sarah's bed and Sarah would hug him and…

Great. Get a grip, he'd told himself. Concentrate on Lucy's croup.

He wanted an emergency. He wanted more than croup. He wanted to get away from this place, away from this time.

Away from Sarah.

They met over the breakfast table and it was apparent to both of them that neither had slept. Sarah eyed Alistair with care, and was aware that he was eying her right back.

'The dog kept me awake,' she said in defensive tones.

'You could have shut the door.'

'What were you doing looking at my door?'

'I wasn't looking at your door.'

'Right.' They were behaving like a couple of kids, she decided. She poked a piece of toast into the toaster and turned her back on the man. 'What's happening?' she asked, still with her back to him. 'Have you heard anything? Are we getting any decent trackers?'

'There should be people arriving this afternoon,' Alistair told her. 'Barry phoned.'

'Barry phoned?'

'He'll be round here in ten minutes,' Alistair said. 'He knows about the cross-matching of criminal records with locals that we did last night.'

'Yeah, I told him I was going to do it,' she said. 'He is the local police after all.'

'I don't know whether I like him having people's criminal histories,' Alistair told her, and she poked her toast some more and winced. She could see why. Would Hilda's brick-stealing be safe with Barry?

Maybe she was misjudging the man. Officially he had more right to the list than she did—and certainly a lot more than Alistair.

'Did you tell him about Howard?'

'I thought he should discuss any conclusions you'd come to with you and not me,' he told her. 'Actually, I didn't tell him we'd gone through them. I thought it best. He phoned while you were in the shower. He asked whether the list had come through. I told him it had and he said he'd come round to discuss it with you. So there you are. Do you want me to absent myself while you discuss police business?'

'You've probably got a ward round to do.'

'I do,' he said, and she couldn't figure out whether he sounded regretful or relieved. 'And a couple of phone calls to make. I had a case of croup in the night I need to check on.'

'Lucy's mother didn't ring back?'

'Were you eavesdropping?' he asked, and she poked her toast some more. She still had her back to him, and her back was very expressive.

'You talk loud.'

'You listened.'

'Not very much,' she said untruthfully. 'And I certainly wasn't interested.'

What was wrong with her? She was behaving like a ninny. Alistair departed for the hospital, and she sat and ate her toast and waited for Barry and thought she was losing her mind.

She was certainly losing her dignity.

'How soon can I get out of here?' she asked Flotsam, and there was real desperation in her voice. 'I'm going to miss you, boy, but I'm certainly not going to miss your master.'

Liar.

Barry sat at the table and ponderously went through the list. 'It's bloody supposition,' he told her. 'You're saying there's someone out here using this area as a base for bringing in illegals?'

'You're right, it is supposition,' she told him. 'But I can't figure out any other scenario that makes sense.'

'Whoever they are, they've been out in the bush for over two days now,' he said, and there was a certain grim satisfaction in his tone. 'I'm starting to think there's been a falling out among thieves and they're dead. Either that or the blood was there before the plane crashed. Maybe we're chasing our tails and there never was anyone aboard. Maybe the whole thing's a storm in a teacup.'

'But you're still searching?'

'I've got a team of locals out there, but we're wasting our time. They're dead, or they don't want to be found—in which case they can starve to death for all I care—or they didn't exist in the first place.'

'We've got an élite squad coming in later today,' she told him, and he nodded.

'Yeah. I heard you asked for that. I'm telling you it's a waste of time. I've got it on the record that it's your idea and not mine. They'll come, they'll search and find nothing, and then I'll cop it for wasting their time.'

'But if there's people out there—'

'Then they're crims or illegals. Either way—'

'Either way they're people. There's a child—'

'Says you.'

'There's a footprint.'

'Yeah.' He stood up. 'A footprint. So on the basis of a footprint you're costing the force a fortune. Well, everyone will know it was on your say-so that extra resources have been pulled in. Now, if you'll excuse me I've got work to do. I dunno what you're still doing here. As far as I know your job was to tell us how the pilot died. You've done that. Why don't you just take off back to the city and leave this to us?'

She could. Sarah stood on the veranda and watched Barry walk back to the police station and thought, Yeah, she could. She could take the mail plane out of here tonight. She was a forensic pathologist. Barry was right. She'd come to do a job and she'd done it.

She could leave.

The phone rang behind her. She hesitated for a moment—almost tempted to leave it. Almost tempted to do what Barry suggested. Finish. Move on.

She couldn't. There were people at risk here, and despite

what Alistair thought of her—despite what she thought of herself—she cared.

She turned and picked up the phone.

'Sarah?' It was Alistair, and her stomach did a crazy lurch at the sound of his voice. Why did it do that? Why couldn't she achieve better control?

'Yes?'

'I've just got a call from Howard Skinner.'

'The Howard Skinner on the list?'

'That's right.' His voice was clipped and efficient—totally business-like. The kiss last night had been an aberration. Nothing more. He'd moved on. 'He's in trouble.'

'What sort of trouble?'

'By the sound of it he has renal colic,' Alistair told her. 'He's just phoned in saying he can't move for pain. The symptoms sound spot-on for renal colic, and with his history of gout…'

'The uric acid will have caused kidney stones.'

'That's what it sounds like. Anyway, I'm heading out there now. Do you want to come?'

Did she want to come?

This was none of her business. It was Barry who was the policeman. She was the forensic pathologist and her role was clearly delineated.

Or was it? She was a member of the police force and she was deeply concerned.

There was no choice. Of course she wanted to come. It was a heaven-sent chance to talk to someone she was really interested in.

'I'll let Barry know,' she told him. 'Maybe he'll want to come, too.'

'I'm not asking you as a police officer,' Alistair snapped. 'If you want to do any police work then that's a separate issue. I'm asking you as a visiting doctor. I might need help.'

Right. She thought about it. Police sniffing round at this stage might do more harm than good. But as a doctor…

'You're right. I'll leave my badge at home,' she told him. 'I'll come, and I'm only wearing a stethoscope.'

The farm was thirty miles out of town, and the country was some of the most barren farming land Sarah had ever seen. For as far as the eye could see there was red dust, a few straggly ironbarks, and sad-looking windmills that looked as if they'd long given up on their task of trying to eke any moisture from this dusty soil. The wind was rising and tumbleweeds were rolling aimlessly in the wind.

The land up to five miles from the coast was still lush and green. But here...

'The hills act as rain catchment,' Alistair told her. 'Out here the rains haven't come for the past three years.'

'It's dreadful.'

'It won't always be dreadful. That's why the international conglomerates hold on to their properties. There'll be a few years of lean, and then the rains will come and this country will be some of the richest grazing land in Australia. They'll stock it up, make a fortune from it, milk it for all they're worth and then sit back while the dry takes over again.'

'So Howard gets to sit and wait?'

'He'll be doing basic maintenance,' Alistair told her. 'He'll make sure the main buildings aren't vandalised. Once the rains arrive the place comes alive, and no one wants to waste time rebuilding ruined homesteads.'

'But it must be the pits of a life,' Sarah said, staring around her in dismay. 'So lonely...'

'There are people who love it. People who make a lifetime career of it. There's a chap further south who's a really well-known poet. He sits up here, takes a wage for doing minimal maintenance and has all the time in the world for his poetry.' He smiled suddenly with that engaging smile Sarah loved so much. 'Mind, it's pretty bleak poetry. There's not a lot of "hosts of golden daffodils" in this lot.'

'I wandered lonely as a tumbleweed,' she agreed, smiling.

He laughed, and the tension took a backseat again. Sarah found herself relaxing. No, she didn't want to go home, she thought. She wanted to stay here until the case was solved.

She wanted to stay here by Alistair's side for as long as she could.

'Barry wasn't helpful?' Alistair asked, and she had to haul herself back to thinking of something other than the way she was reacting to this man.

'Barry's appalling.'

'So put in a report when you get back.' Alistair grimaced. 'We need to get rid of him.'

'You won't get rid of him unless he puts a foot wrong. And he won't.'

'I hope he won't,' Alistair said grimly. 'The man's a loose cannon. I don't trust him.'

'He's all you have.'

'Yeah.' He cast her a sideways glance. 'He's all I have. And it's not much at all.'

The homestead was surprisingly pleasant. Alistair's truck bumped over the cattle grid, and she saw there were trees lining a long driveway. They were poor excuses for trees, but they were trees for all that, and there was even the semblance of a garden around the long, low house.

'Howard will be using bore water to keep the trees alive,' Alistair told her. 'When the rains come it's important to get competent staff, and they won't come if the place isn't good.'

'So Howard won't get to stay?'

'No, but he knows that. They all do. People usually have a reason for doing what he's doing.'

'It'd work,' she said slowly, staring at the outbuildings. Everywhere looked deserted, but by the look of the small cottages scattered around the main homestead the place was built to accommodate half a dozen families. 'As a base for accommodating people while they process papers—teaching them rudiments of language—sorting places for them to go— it'd be perfect.'

'You really are serious?'

'How many people come out here?' she asked, and Alistair shrugged.

'No one.'

'There's an airstrip.' She looked over at the back of the house, where a windsock was waving wildly in the wind. 'I'd like to see if it's been used recently.'

'We need to see to Howard.'

'Yeah. Medicine first.' She grimaced. 'Okay, I've put the handcuffs away for the moment. Let's play doctors.'

They needed to play doctors. Howard was in real trouble.

Renal colic was something that was commonly used as a ruse by drug addicts to get young and unsuspecting doctors to prescribe strong narcotics. It was a good fake diagnosis, as kidney stones caused pain that was well-nigh unbearable. The pain was distinctive, crippling, running from the loin into the groin. So drug addicts often arrived at emergency rooms screaming, doubling over in pain, swearing that they'd had kidney stones before.

But an experienced doctor could usually tell if it was real, and it wasn't hard now.

Howard was doubled up on a bed in the back of the house. When they found him he looked up at them with eyes that were despairing.

He was a slight man in his late forties or early fifties, lean, weathered and hollow-eyed with shock. His face was drenched in sweat, he felt clammy, and his pulse-rate was up to a hundred and ten.

All symptoms almost impossible to fake.

'I'll give you some morphine straight away,' Alistair told him. 'Then we'll get you into hospital.'

'I don't want to go to hospital.' It was a whispered plea.

'You can't stay here,' Alistair told him. 'It's the same problem that's causing your gout. A build-up of uric acid.' He was injecting morphine as he spoke. 'Now the uric acid will have caused stones. We need to do something about them.'

'Operate?'

'If we're lucky the stone will pass by itself. But you need a urologist, Howard. We'll take you back to Dolphin Cove. I'll watch for a couple of days, but if you don't pass them then we'll arrange an air ambulance to take you to Cairns.'

'I can't leave,' he gasped. 'I can't.'

'The place is dead quiet,' Alistair said firmly. 'You don't have a choice.' He signalled to Sarah, who was standing behind him. 'This is Dr Rose, who's assisting me for a few days. Dr Rose will back me up.'

'I will.' Sarah gave the man a sympathetic smile. All she had on this man were vague suspicions, and she could certainly be sympathetic until they were confirmed. And even if they were confirmed, a sentence of renal colic was cruel. 'The good news is that renal colic is easily treatable,' she told him. 'You may well pass the stones in the next couple of days and be able to come straight home again.'

'You're a doctor, too?'

'Sarah's doing a bit of training with me for the next few days,' Alistair told him. 'She's a city doctor—never seen places like this.'

'Yeah?' The man was too intent on his pain to care. 'Can't you just give me something to stop the pain here?'

'I can. I am. But in four hours you'll need more.'

'I don't want to be stuck in hospital.'

'Tell you what,' Alistair said, appearing to think it through. 'You have a car here? What if I take you back in my truck— it's set up so you can lie comfortably in the back—and Dr Rose follows us in your car. Then when you want to leave you can. If you pass the stone tonight you can come straight home.'

The man was trying to think. They could see the effort it took. Renal colic was one of the worst types of pain and the morphine hadn't kicked in yet. Maybe Alistair should have waited until the painkillers took effect before planning, Sarah thought, but then she thought, No.

She was under no illusion. Alistair had suggested this plan for a reason.

'Tell us where your house and car keys are,' Alistair told him. 'I'll get you straight into hospital—get you comfortable. Dr Rose can lock up here and bring in your car in behind us.'

Howard stared up, desperation clearly written in his face. He looked from Alistair to Sarah and back again.

'She's a city doctor?' he said doubtfully.

'I can drive,' Sarah said, in a voice that said she was a little bit unsure—maybe a little younger than she was—a little less confident. Certainly nothing like as confident as a police forensic pathologist should be. 'If you think I can manage, Dr Benn?'

'I think you can manage,' Alistair told her. He turned back to the man on the bed and Sarah could see that he was trying to hide a smile. 'She's a real newbie,' he told Howard. 'But I think we can trust her to drive a car. Just go really slowly, Sarah, and don't take any risks.'

'No, Dr Benn.'

The thing was done.

Which was how Sarah stood on the veranda, watching Alistair's truck disappear in the distance, holding the keys to the homestead in her hand. All the keys.

She looked down at them and grinned.

'I won't take any risks at all,' she murmured.

'Is she following?'

Howard was stretched out on the permanent bed Alistair used as often as not to transport patients. Dolphin Cove did have an ambulance, but it was old and rickety and usually it was less trouble for Alistair to use the Land Cruiser. He'd made Howard as comfortable as possible and, with the morphine kicking in, Howard was now able to think of something other than his pain. His brain might be woozy from the drug, but he obviously didn't like the idea that he'd left someone behind with his keys.

Alistair nodded to himself. Maybe Sarah was right. Maybe Howard did have something to worry about. But he could reassure him. He looked in the rearview mirror as though he expected to see her and sighed and shook his head.

'Nope. And I wouldn't expect it.' Alistair turned his truck onto the main road. 'Speed is not our Dr Rose's strong point. She'll probably be trying to fit the front door key in the ignition of your car.'

'She's not real bright?' Howard asked, obviously relieved at the thought.

Alistair appeared to think about it. 'Let's just say she's not your ideal family doctor,' he said at last. 'To be honest,' he confessed to Howard, 'I don't mind if she does take a while. She's come up to the country for a stint of country medicine and she's driving me nuts. I'll be pleased to be shot of her for a while.'

'That's okay.' Howard lay back and relaxed. A dopey female doctor posed no threat at all. 'That's great.'

The dopey female doctor was being anything but dopey. Left on her own at the deserted homestead, she prepared to take every advantage. Aware that she really couldn't be more than half an hour behind Alistair without questions being raised, she worked fast.

First she headed for the airstrip—and there was the first of her questions answered. Although there was no aeroplane present, and the building obviously used as a hangar was empty, the strip had had been recently used. It must have rained a little recently—there were the first faint tinges of green shoots—but along a strip in the centre of the runway the shoots had been broken off. There was a dusty patch near the house—signs of people gathering, staying for a while in the one place?

The strip was used.

Maybe the owners came and visited. There was nothing illegal in that.

The homestead?

She looked at the house Howard had come from and decided against it. Instead she made her way to the first of the little cottages. They were obviously used for the workmen who ran this station in bustling times. Alistair had said that those times were at least three years past.

The bundle of keys in her hand was like a jigsaw. It took her five minutes of frustrated fiddling before she found the key to the first cottage, and by then she was growing nervous. The wind was whistling eerily around the buildings. She was intensely aware of being alone.

I'm a doctor, not a detective, she told herself—but she still wanted to see. And Alistair had given her the opportunity.

The key clicked into place. She walked in. And stopped.

The place was set up for human habitation. This was not somewhere that hadn't been used for three years.

It was Spartan—two bedrooms opening from a central living room, and each bedroom holding two sets of double bunks. Each bed had a pile of folded linen and blankets at the foot—army issue grey. Nothing fancy. Serviceable.

Three beds had linen.

She stared at them, and then looked into the kitchenette.

A box of groceries lay on the bench. She walked over and checked it out. Dried milk. Biscuits. Dry pasta. Tinned meat and vegetables. Baked beans.

Sugar, coffee, tea.

There was a refrigerator, and the hum indicated it was operating. She swung the door wide.

Butter. And the freezer held bread. She checked the use-by date of the bread.

It had been bought a week ago.

She stood and stared around her. The place looked unused now, but it looked—expectant. Waiting.

Were the people in the back of the plane supposed to be

coming here? Were they even now trying to make their way here?

A scratch at the door made her start. She whirled around. A tumbleweed had hurled itself at the screen door in the wind. It rolled against the flywire, was caught by another gust and was gone.

She'd never make a detective, Sarah decided. She'd turn to jelly in a minute.

She needed to concentrate. Fast. What now?

There was a folder on the table. Sarah walked forward and flipped it open with the tip of a finger.

Three passports. Australian passports.

No photographs.

She flicked each open in turn and read.

Amal Inor. Male. Aged thirty-five.

Noa Inor. Female. Aged thirty-six.

Azron Inor. Male. Aged five.

No photographs. The section for photographs was missing. These passports were waiting to be collected—by whoever was in the plane.

Mother, father and son? Amal, Noa and Azron.

Five years old?

'Where are you?' It was a faint whisper. She found she was staring down at the passports as if she could see their owners. All she saw was that tiny, bloody footprint.

'Where are you?' she whispered again, but nobody answered. If anyone was to find the answer it had to be her.

I need to find Barry, she told herself. And Alistair.

Why did she have more confidence in Alistair than she did in the local police force?

CHAPTER SEVEN

SERGEANT BARRY WATKINS was fretting. There were ten members of an élite police squad due to arrive in town in four hours and he was nervous.

He'd done everything right—hadn't he? He'd spent half his time out at the wreck scene searching, and he still had a group of locals organised there now. Not that they'd find anything.

He'd thought it through. Something had happened in that plane, that much he could tell, but it might have happened anywhere. The pilot was a dope addict. What was the bet there'd been a fight in the back of the plane at some time? Some time past. Some time when the plane had been off his patch. There was nothing to say when the blood had been spilled.

All the same…

If there were criminals out there it'd look so much better if he found them. But spending the day scouring the stinking hot country near the wreck wasn't his scene.

Maybe it'd be better if he was out there when the search party arrived, though, he thought. Maybe.

He thought about it and decided he was right. But it was so hot. If he was going to go he'd go down to the general store, buy himself a packet of fags and a few bottles of water. He'd pack the backpack with the medical kit so it looked like he was expecting to find someone. Yeah.

He'd just go down to the store now and then head straight out to the wreck.

Alistair settled Howard into the ward. He rang the urologist in Cairns and wrote up orders for morphine, but there was little else he could do.

'Stones usually pass of their own accord,' the urologist told him. 'I'd advise you to sit on him for a couple of days before you send him on to Cairns. Keep an eye on his urine—the stones may well fragment themselves and come loose. Check for blood in the urine. Keep the pain under control. Give me a ring tomorrow and let me know what's happening.'

Fine. And that was fine with Howard, too. Or, at least, it was better than going to Cairns. He didn't even want to be in hospital. 'Just give me painkillers,' he whispered, his voice fuzzy from the drugs he'd been given. 'I want to go home.'

'I can't give you morphine unless you're in hospital, and until the stones pass nothing else will keep it under control. Can you cope with that pain on your own?'

'No, but…'

'Do you want to go to Cairns?'

'No!'

'Then settle back and accept a couple of days' enforced rest,' Alistair told him.

'My car…'

'Sarah's bringing it in. I'll go and check if she's here, shall I?'

'Yeah,' Howard told him. 'That'd be good.' He closed his eyes and thought about it…for about two seconds before he stopped thinking about anything at all. After a night of agony, sleep was all Howard was going to think about for a long time.

Sarah drove down the main street of Dolphin Cove and, on impulse, drew to a stop outside the general store. Howard had bought those groceries here. How often did he buy those sort of packs? she wondered. It was a clearly defined set of items—bigger than one man would go through. If she found a helpful storekeeper he might be able to recall Howard's spending patterns.

Maybe this wasn't the first time this had happened. Maybe there'd been more people in the past. There was something about the cottage she'd just been in that spoke of organisation. It hinted at more than one group of people coming in and out.

There were so many questions. Shopping patterns might well answer one of them.

If there were wounded people… Time was so short.

She could but ask.

Howard's car wasn't in the hospital car park. Alistair glanced at his watch and felt a sharp stab of unease. Surely she should be here by now? It had seemed like a good idea to leave Sarah at the property alone so she could have a good poke around, but now…

He gazed along the main street and gave a sigh of relief. Here was Howard's car—a distinctive yellow Ford—coming now.

No. It wasn't coming here. She was stopping at the general store.

Why was she stopping? She'd know Howard would be nervous. She wouldn't know that he'd fall asleep so fast.

He glanced at his watch. He had fifteen minutes before he was due in clinic. He might just walk down and meet her.

Desperation drove people to do things they'd never dream of doing in their lives. Amal had never before stolen so much as a loaf of bread. He wouldn't have dreamt of doing so. But he had no currency. Nothing. His family were starving and Azron was so ill…

So what else could he do?

'If they catch you before you have the necessary papers they'll deport you straight away,' he'd been told. 'They don't care what happens to you and your families. They'll send you straight back to the authorities. You'll be killed.'

He would be killed. He knew that for a fact. Dr Amal Inor was deemed a state criminal.

He hadn't always been so. Of course he hadn't. And that he was a criminal now seemed unthinkable. A successful and caring family doctor, Amal remembered with awful clarity the night when he'd become one—the night only seven weeks ago when he'd been woken abruptly from sleep. There'd been an assassination attempt on the head of the political opposition—a learned old cleric in his seventies—and it was only too clear who'd ordered the assassination.

No matter who had ordered the killing, it had gone awry. The old man hadn't been killed. Dreadfully wounded, he'd been dragged to Amal's house by his terrified friends. Why? Because Amal was known to be good-hearted. It was known everywhere that he was kind. The men had been sure that Amal would never turn anyone away.

They'd been right. Amal hadn't been able to refuse, despite knowing the dreadful cost. So Amal had treated the old man, knowing in his heart that this was the end.

The man had survived, to be spirited out of the country. And Amal had fled too. He'd had no choice. He'd gathered what he could, paid the price demanded by the black marketeers who organised people-smuggling, and when they had finally come for him—as he had known they would—his house was deserted.

Amal and his wife and son were on their way to Australia.

Australia. To horror upon horror. To this.

How long could they survive? He didn't know. All he knew was that he had to try.

He'd been watching the store for an hour now. People walked in, made their purchases and walked out. There was a petrol pump out at the front. The owner came out periodically to pump petrol. He stood at the petrol pumps and he gossiped, as if he had all the time in the world.

Amal had gone behind the building to check. There was a back door. If he was fast…

Dear heaven, he'd never done anything like this in his life. What turned a man into a criminal?

Desperation. He had no choice.

*   *   *

Max Hogg, owner of Dolphin Cove's general store, was fed up with standing behind the counter, and when he saw Sarah pull up out front he strolled out to meet her. He knew who she was—the whole town knew who she was and what she was here for. Max was therefore delighted to meet her.

He was even more delighted—and intrigued—by her questions. Sure he could help her. He had all the time in the world. Now, when had he last seen Howard…?

Barry didn't have all the time in the world. He was anxious and angry and the last person he wanted to see was Sarah. As he walked down the street towards them Max kept on talking to her, as if he couldn't even see Barry.

'I need some bottled water,' he interrupted, and Sarah turned and smiled at him. It was a placatory smile, but Barry didn't see it like that.

'I need to talk to you, Barry,' she told him, and he shrugged.

'Later. I'm busy. Max, can you get me the water now?'

'Sure thing, Barry,' Max told him with easy geniality. 'Hey, it's a party. Here's Dr Benn. Hi, Alistair. Can you keep Dr Rose amused while I go and serve Barry?'

'Of course.' Alistair walked up the steps of the shop's veranda to join Sarah as Max and Barry walked inside the shop together.

And then all hell broke loose.

There was Max's voice, raised in confusion. 'Stop! Hey, stop! You haven't paid for that. Where do you think you're going? Barry!'

And then Barry. 'What the…?'

Max again. 'He's pinching stuff. He's—'

And, worst of all, Barry's voice, raised in warning—'Stop. This is the police. Stop now or I'll shoot. Last warning… Stop or I'll shoot. Now!'

The sound of gunfire split the hot sleepy afternoon as nothing else could. Alistair and Sarah gazed at each other for a fraction of a horrified moment.

And ran.

The man had stopped, but not of his own volition.

Out at the back of the store, in the centre of the dusty side lane leading from the storeroom to the road, he lay sprawled face down in the dirt. A pile of groceries was flung every which way about him.

They reached him together, Alistair and Sarah, while Max stood open-mouthed in horrified amazement and Barry stared down at his gun as if he couldn't believe it had just done what it had.

As Alistair stooped over the figure Barry seemed to haul himself together. He took a step forward. The gun was aimed again. 'Careful,' he snapped. 'He might be armed.'

Alistair simply ignored him. There was a spreading bloom of crimson over the man's upper spine. Alistair's fingers were on the man's neck. Searching.

Sarah was down in the dust beside him.

'He's alive.' Alistair looked up at Max, fiercely urgent, knowing instinctively that Max would be more use than Barry. 'Max, hit the emergency number. Tell Claire I want the emergency cart down here now. Then get someone to bring my truck. The keys are in the nurses' station. Move.'

Max was a big man, but he wasn't slow. He took one searing, gulping breath—and moved.

'Pressure,' Alistair said, moving his palm to the source of blood and pressing down. 'We need to stop the flow before we turn him. Hell, it's pumping.'

'Use this.' Sarah had seen the oozing blood and her T-shirt was already over her head and folded into a wad. As she brought it over the wound Alistair lifted his hand. She placed the pad over and pushed. Then, as she applied as much pressure as she could, Alistair gently felt underneath him.

'There's an exit wound,' he told her. 'It's bleeding, too,

but not pumping. I'll pressure it from underneath. Barry, grab more wadding. Cloth—anything.'

'He didn't stop,' Barry said stupidly, and Sarah closed her eyes in frustration. She was fighting blood flow here. Desperately. She wanted help—not explanations.

'Here.' It was Max, back again with a speed that was almost stunning. He had a handful of teatowels and Sarah opened her eyes again and looked up with real gratitude. 'Claire's on her way with whoever she can find,' Max told them. 'Has he killed him?'

'He'll be lucky,' Sarah said grimly. Blood was oozing between her fingers and she pushed harder. 'Max, help me here. I want a tighter wad. Can you fold me one?'

'Sure.'

They worked desperately. The most urgent thing was to stop the bleeding. At least slow it. More pressure…

And then Claire arrived, breathless, carting a huge bag. This town might be on its own medically, but in an emergency the population moved faster than any city emergency team Sarah had ever seen.

'I need an IV line,' Alistair told Claire, not bothering with explanations, not even bothering to look up. From the amount of blood Claire could see what most needed to be done, and explanations took a poor second in the list of their priorities. 'Sarah, have you got that bleeding under control?'

She couldn't press any harder. 'I think so.'

'Then we risk rolling him.'

A man Sarah recognised as the hospital orderly appeared then. He was carrying a stretcher, and Alistair signalled for it to be laid beside the stranger.

'Okay,' he told them. 'Max, can you help us here? We roll over really, really slowly, so that Sarah's pad's not dislodged. Four of us rolling, keeping him rigid, keeping the pressure on his side. I want his shoulders kept in a straight line as he rolls. Sarah, keep your hand on the wound, keep pressing, and don't stop. This way we get to see the damage to his chest and he gets to be on the stretcher. One, two... Now!'

They rolled.

Sarah's hand moved with him so her fingers were caught under his back, still pressing.

They could see him fully now. He lay on the stretcher, staring up as Alistair worked over him.

Who was he?

He was a small man, in his late thirties or early forties, Sarah thought. Maybe Middle Eastern? He had a gentle face, she thought, though it was now haggard and unshaven— filthy—as if he hadn't seen a wash for weeks.

His eyes were wide and pain filled.

He was conscious?

'Keep still,' Alistair told him, and he closed his eyes.

'Do you understand us?' Sarah asked, and got an almost imperceptible nod.

'We're doctors,' she told him. She was still concentrating on maintaining pressure, and with her hand underneath him she wasn't free to do anything else. Alistair had Claire pressing on the chest wound—the bullet had obviously left an entry and exit wound—and he was fixing an IV line. They needed to get fluids in fast. Saline. Plasma.

But was it any use? Sarah stared down at the chest wound and thought about where her fingers were feeling the pumping blood. Mentally she tracked the bullet's path. Not heart. Thank God, not heart. But lung. It had to have hit lung.

The man's eyes flickered open again. They found hers and she searched for an explanation. What explanation was there when he'd been shot for stealing...what? Loaves of bread?

She had to try.

'We're trying to help you,' she said gently. They'd move him fast, but not before Alistair had done what was needed to try and stabilise him. He had the IV line in place and was searching in his bag for the oxygen mask. The orderly behind him had brought an oxygen cylinder.

The man's eyes were on Sarah.

'It was a mistake to shoot you,' she said softly. 'A dreadful mistake. We want to help you now. Do you understand?'

Once more, a tiny nod. He understood English, then. He was wearing trousers that must once have been neat, and a shirt that once might even have been a business shirt. His black brogues were coated with dust.

'Azron,' he whispered, in a voice that was thickly accented. 'Help…Azron.'

'Is Azron your son?' she asked.

Alistair had an oxygen mask ready to put over his face, but Sarah gave an urgent shake of her head. The man's need for oxygen was imperative, but there was another imperative that had to be considered. She thought back bleakly to the amount of blood she'd seen in the plane. Someone else was in trouble.

'Yes.'

'Where can we find him?'

'Not…' The man stared at her with eyes that were glazing with shock and with pain. 'Not…' He looked past her and his eyes rested on Barry. Barry who stood at a loss behind them, uniformed, his hand still holding his gun.

'Not find,' he whispered, and closed his eyes.

They loaded him into Alistair's truck and closed the doors. Alistair and Sarah stayed in the back with him—Sarah was still acting as a human pressure pad and she couldn't shift. Max drove.

'I'll report this,' Barry said grimly, and Alistair winced.

'You do that. Just stay out of my way.'

Claire moved forward to close the doors on them, and as she did Sarah looked backward. And frowned.

Had she imagined it?

Nothing.

Or…was it?

A wisp of cloth behind the buildings. A fleeting glimpse.

She almost called out. Almost. But Barry was still there. His hand was still on his gun.

She'd imagined it. She must have.

Amal groaned and she turned her attention to him. To imperatives.

They came so close to losing him—but somehow they didn't. Somehow they succeeded.

For the next two hours Sarah and Alistair worked with the desperation of people who knew that their best efforts might well be in vain. The wound was dreadful.

The bullet had tracked in through the right lung. The gaping, sucking wound in the man's back was whistling with air as well as blood. By the time they reached the hospital Sarah could feel the man's trachea shifting to the side. The pressure of one collapsing lung, with air build-up in the cavity outside the lung in the chest wall, was causing everything else to shift, to shut down. Tension pneumothorax...

'We need to put in a chest drain,' she told Alistair as she listened to his chest. 'I can't.'

'I can,' he told her. 'At least I think I can. I have the equipment. I've seen it done.'

'I've read about it,' she told him, and he gave a rueful grimace.

'There you go, then. What a team. What are we waiting for?'

What were they waiting for? Expertise, she thought bleakly. That was what they urgently wanted here.

Expertise was in short supply. They were all this man had. They were all that stood between this man and death.

What had Sarah been told? She thought back to the publican's blunt assessment of the situation.

'We're a one-doctor town. We know that. It's a risk we take.'

The locals accepted that they had one doctor here and that in an emergency he might not be able to cope.

It was bad enough, but to have such a situation with a gun-happy cop...

'What did you say to him before he lost consciousness?'

Alistair asked. He was fighting to put together equipment and waiting for a call he'd put through to Cairns to get some emergency on-line assistance from a specialist surgeon. Sarah was adjusting oxygen—the man needed more, but his lungs were losing capacity all the time.

'He was frightened for his son.'

'His son?'

'Out at the farm I found three forged Australian passports prepared for Amal Inor, his wife Noa, and his five-year-old son Azron. I figure this guy must be Amal. He talked about his son. Azron. Which confirms it. I asked him where they were, but Barry was there. He was too frightened.'

Alistair grimaced. 'Even if he pulls through we're not going to be able to talk to him.'

'No. We had that one opportunity. And because of Barry…'

'Barry's out of here,' Alistair told her. 'Even if I have to run the guy out of town myself.'

They took X-rays, confirming air in the right thorax. They cross-matched blood for transfusion and Alistair contacted locals with the same group. 'They're used to it,' he told Sarah. 'This is a small community. There's never any trouble getting blood donors—everyone knows they may need it themselves some day.' Then, with the assistance of a specialist thoracic surgeon, teleconferencing from Cairns, they managed the next step.

A chest tube was inserted into the chest cavity using a local anaesthetic.

Their patient was drifting in and out of consciousness. There was no way Sarah was risking a general anaesthetic, and he didn't need it. Alistair had administered so much morphine he'd hardly even need the local anaesthetic she did administer.

Then she watched as Alistair carefully inserted what was needed. The trocar and cannula consisted of an outer tube inserted right into the chest, with a tiny valved suction tube inserted in the centre. Once in position, the outer tube was withdrawn, leaving the inner tube in place. The tube was connected to an underwater seal, which allowed the air leaking from the damaged lung to exit through the tube but no air back again.

The intention was to seal the lung. It would let the man breathe until more permanent repairs could be made.

And, blessedly, it worked. The tube in place, they could concentrate on stopping the bleeding.

The wound was a gaping mess. He'd need specialist surgery to repair it completely—he needed to be moved to Cairns—but they had to get him stable first. They worked on, and by the time Alistair stood back from the table Sarah was as exhausted as Alistair looked.

'That's it.' Alistair's whole body seemed to slump. 'We've done all we can.'

'He has a chance,' Sarah whispered.

Alistair nodded. 'A good chance. I think. Barring complications.' He lifted the man's hand and held it in his. 'What did you say his name was?'

'Amal. As I said, it's a guess, but I think I'm right.'

He nodded. 'Amal, can you hear us?'

Amal's eyes fluttered open. He looked at them with eyes that were cloudy from drugs and pain and shock.

'Amal, you're safe now.' Alistair's voice gentled as he realised the man was taking in what he was being told. 'You're safe. But we need to find your family. Can you help us?'

Amal gazed up at them some more. He simply looked. Nothing.

'Amal?'

There was a weak shake of the head. A tear appeared at the corner of the man's right eye and trickled down his dusty cheek.

He closed his eyes.

This wasn't sleep, Sarah thought. He wasn't sleeping. He wasn't telling them anything.

He was still terrified. If they had shot him, imagine what they could do to his precious wife and son.

'I'll kill him.'

She'd never seen him this angry. Sarah followed Alistair out to the sinks, then stood back and watched as he hauled off his gown and turned the taps on full. Water spurted out of the faucet so hard it hit the bottom and burst up again, splashing over his shoes. He didn't appear to notice. He'd held himself under rigid control while he was operating, she realised, but now combined tension and rage were threatening to overwhelm him.

'He wasn't armed.' Alistair's voice was a cold whisper. 'He was carrying armloads of food and he was running away. Barry could have caught him. If he'd run he could have caught him. And he stands there like a moron and shoots...he shoots...'

Sarah walked forward and eased the taps back. His gown had caught—one of the ties was still fastened and the green fabric was still hanging uselessly around his waist. She undid the tie and let the thing fall.

'Alistair...'

'People.' He finished washing and turned, staring blindly at her, so frustrated with rage that he hardly saw her. Or rather he did see her. And what he saw he didn't like. 'Stupid, irresponsible people. You damage and you damage and you damage...'

Was he talking about her?

'Life's so precious, and you don't realise... Blasting like that with a gun—for a few loaves of bread! Taking drugs and getting behind a wheel...'

Yep, it seemed they were talking about her. Sarah's face closed.

'The police squad from Cairns has arrived,' she said bleakly. 'I need to talk to them before Barry cements his own version of events in their heads.' She motioned to the cellphone on her belt. 'Call me if you need me. Medical emergencies only.'

And she walked away before her own anger overwhelmed her. Before she could do what she really wanted to do.

Which was to hit him from here to the middle of next week. Hit someone.

Barry? Yes.

Alistair? Him, too.

The helicopter that had brought the police squad from Cairns was used to evacuate Amal. They were desperate to speak to him, but his life hung on him getting specialist treatment. If they kept him in Dolphin Cove he'd maybe be able to tell them something that would let them find his wife and son, but his damaged lung required surgery immediately. There wasn't a choice.

So he went. Sarah stood on the veranda and watched the helicopter take off and thought she could have been on it.

She should have been on it. Her work here was done. For Sarah, who'd spent the last six years carefully not getting involved, it had been a prime opportunity for her to say, Amal needs medical attention during the flight and I'm offering to go with him. You don't need me any more. I'm out of here.

But the helicopter that had brought the team had been used also to transfer someone else. An old man, a native of one of the inland settlements, who had been in Cairns for treatment for a tumour that had finally been termed inoperable. His doctors had been waiting for an opportunity to transport him back, to spend his last few weeks with his people, so the huge transport helicopter had also been carrying his doctor and a nurse.

There were therefore medical personnel already on board for the trip back to Cairns. They'd look after Amal.

And no one had suggested Sarah go, too. She'd found herself fading as much as she could into the background, as though she was afraid someone would suddenly turn and say, What are you doing here? Why don't you leave?

Her job had been to come and determine how the pilot had died. She'd done that. There were detectives here now. Police who knew more about finding fugitives than she did.

'What am I doing?' She stooped and hugged Flotsam, who seemed entirely happy to be hugged. It was as if the little dog sensed her need and was pleased to oblige. 'Alistair hates me. I don't know what that kiss was about. It was crazy. He just hates me. And I…'

What was she feeling? She knew what she was feeling, and it was all about that kiss. Which was crazy.

She should go home. There was nothing here for her.

There was nothing at home for her.

'I've stuffed it so badly,' she said bleakly. 'All I can do…all I can do, Flotsam, is see if I can redeem myself somehow. Where are Noa and Azron? If I could find them, if I could help in some way… There has to be something I can do.'

She thought of that wisp of cloth she'd seen back at the shop as she'd helped load Amal into the truck-cum-ambulance. Did it have any significance? Probably not, she thought, but she could go down and have a look. She could see if there was anything there that could explain it.

'You're making excuses to stay,' she told herself fiercely. 'You think there's anything you can do that will make any difference?'

Of course there wasn't. She was clutching at straws.

It wouldn't make any difference at all.

'To me, no,' she told the little dog. 'But maybe it'll make a difference to Noa and Azron.'

Yeah, right.

She couldn't help it. She hugged the little dog closer and knew that she had no choice. She was staying.

Like it or not, Sarah was involved. Right up to her heart.

Alistair watched the helicopter fade into the distance and he turned to the head of the police squad with a heavy heart. He was feeling sick. He should have prevented it. He knew Barry was a loose cannon. He should have pushed…

But he had to focus now on what lay ahead. The helicopter had brought back-up—a crack force of eight, with authority, intelligence and purpose. At least now they had some real help.

'We've taken Barry off active duty pending an enquiry,' he was told.

Larry, the head of the police team, had heard an outline of what had happened and was looking grave himself. News of the shooting would surely hit the national press. The last thing the Australian police force wanted was to be seen as gun-happy. And for one of their number to shoot unnecessarily, when he already had a record for unwarranted force…

There'd be questions right to the top.

'It's too late now,' Alistair said, but the man beside him shook his head.

'The prognosis is hopeful.' Larry Giles was a senior detective with the Federal Police. He was good at his job and he'd spent time this morning and on the flight here getting up to speed on this case. By the time he landed he'd already been briefed by the consultant who'd talked Alistair through the operation and who'd be taking over Amal's care back in Cairns.

A lot depended on Amal's surviving. Larry hadn't put pressure on—not exactly—but he knew Amal would get the very best medical care available to anyone. 'All we need to do now is find the rest of his family,' he told Alistair.

The man obviously had more confidence than Alistair felt.

'The rest—whoever they are—are wounded,' he said heavily. 'And Sarah's sure there's a child.'

'If Sarah says there's a child there'll be a child,' Larry told him. 'She's good. With her remaining here we have an excellent medical team. We have decent trackers and we've brought a couple of sniffer dogs. We'll work fast. We're giving it our best shot.'

'Sarah's staying?' He hadn't really thought about her leaving, but now… Why didn't she leave? If she left then maybe he could relax.

But it wasn't to be.

'For the time being I've asked that she stay,' Larry told him. 'I've worked with her before. She's the best police doctor we have. I understand she's been more than useful already.'

'Yeah.' Alistair's response was no more than a grunt, and Larry gave him a curious look.

'Is there a problem?'

'No.' Alistair gave a weary shake of his head. 'No problem at all.'

Washing. It was nothing but laundry. Plus an over-vivid imagination.

Sarah stood where she'd stood earlier and stared at the fluttering line of laundry in the backyard next to the shop. There were sheets flapping in the wind. While she watched, a corner of the sheet whipped up and fluttered against the corner of the fence.

That was what she'd seen. It must have been. She was getting so desperate she was imagining things.

Damn. She stared at it with hopeless eyes. She was so weary she was almost asleep on her feet. She hadn't been able to sleep here. She was so confused.

She was useless.

In the yard next to Max's store, Mariette Hardy carried her second load of washing out into her backyard and started pegging it out. There'd been so much going on today she was running way behind. Her second son had some sort of tummy bug—he'd been ill now for two days, and she was starting to worry. On top of that there'd been the shooting next door. So upsetting.

But the washing had to be done. She'd changed Donny's

sheets twice today already. If she hadn't known Alistair was busy she'd have taken him in to see him. But she'd give Donny another night before she called for medical help, she thought. If she had enough sheets.

She started pegging and then she faltered. There was too much room on the line.

There was a sheet missing.

Where was it?

It was windy. Hadn't she pegged it hard enough?

She put her nose over the fence into the backyard of Max's shop. Sometimes her washing ended up there.

Nothing. All she could see was a pool of blood where Amal's body had lain.

She winced. Ugh.

Maybe it'd blown over and they'd used it, she thought, and good luck to them if they had. A sheet wasn't a great price to pay for a man's life. It might have helped keep the poor man alive.

She shrugged. She wouldn't enquire, she decided. The police had enough on their minds without worrying about one sheet, and she had enough on her mind worrying about Donny.

Mariette went back to her laundry.

Up in the hills behind the town Noa cradled her son and she wept. She'd rewrapped his wound as best she could, in torn pieces of the clean sheet, but she didn't have the knowledge to do more. He was feverish.

His father would know what to do.

Amal.

His father was dying. Maybe he was already dead.

No. She refused to believe it. The girl—the woman with the bright red hair—what had she said?

'We're doctors. We're trying to help you.'

She'd hardly been able to see them. She'd kept back—

Amal hadn't known that she'd followed, but she'd been so fearful. So fearful.

We're doctors. We're trying to help you.

Could she believe it?

No. She could believe no one. Trust no one. Not any more.

And Amal was no longer capable of helping. There was only Noa between her son and death. Amal had done what he must and now it was her turn.

She ran her fingers through her little son's soft curls, and with her other hand she cradled her last hope.

The cold, grim comfort of a small and ugly pistol.

CHAPTER EIGHT

SHE might be feeling useless and exhausted, but Sarah had no wish to go home. After staring at Mariette's washing, acting on impulse, Sarah called into Max's store.

She found him distraught. 'If he needed the stuff so badly I would have given it to him,' he told her, and she believed him.

And here at least she could be useful. In Sarah Max found someone he could use to debrief. She spent almost an hour with him, and by the end of it, as well as carrying home an armload of ingredients for a decent dinner, she also carried away information about Howard's shopping habits. What he'd told her cemented her impressions. Howard was in this up to his neck.

Howard might well know who these people were. He had their passports prepared and waiting. Maybe he knew their backgrounds.

Back at the hospital, she went to search for Larry. The team were starting out at dawn to begin their sweeping search of the area, and they'd taken over the pub as accommodation, but they were using the hospital meeting room as a base.

She found Larry with Alistair. She walked in and one glance told her that Alistair was feeling as uncomfortable as she was. The atmosphere between them was dreadful—what he'd said was rolling over and over in her mind, making her sick at heart. Comparing her to Barry…

'I'm sorry. Am…am I interrupting?'

'No.' They'd been sitting at the big meeting room table, used for an assortment of community health meetings, but as soon as he saw her Alistair was on his feet. 'I was just going.'

'There's no need.'

'I have work to do.'

Right. Of course. His leaving should make her feel better. It didn't.

Somehow, with him gone, she gave a stiff, faltering account of what she'd learned, and if Larry, who had worked with her often before, found her demeanour strange he obviously put it down to the events of the afternoon. They'd been enough to shake anyone. Sarah's work was usually in the aftermath of crime. Not in the forefront.

'You think this is part of some systematic scheme?' Larry demanded, and Sarah nodded.

'The place is set up out there to receive people, and it looks like it's been done professionally. There was equipment for taking passport photographs. There were clothes. There were blank passport books.'

'It makes more and more sense,' Larry said grimly. 'We've been looking at people-smuggling for a while. We've come across a few people who've used black market means to get here. They've all paid an absolute fortune to get here and then been dumped in the cities with nothing. All of them say they were brought initially to some remote farm that none could describe. And the worst thing is that nearly all of them are genuine refugees. They've taken the black market option because of panic. They had reason to panic, but if they'd been pointed to the correct authorities they would have been helped without payment. Someone's making a fortune out of their desperation.'

He rose, purpose in his face. Sarah knew this man well. Larry was a big man, with a ruthless exterior, but inside he was as soft as putty. Sarah had seen him deal with the worst type of criminals and she knew he didn't hold back. But when he needed to be gentle...there was a core of humanity in the man that made his pursuit of the criminal element take on a dimension not often seen in a man in such a position.

'I need to talk to your Howard,' he told her, and Sarah nodded.

'Do you want me to come with you?'

'I'll ask Alistair. He's the charge doctor. It'd look better on the reports.'

She nodded.

'Are you getting on okay with Dr Benn?' Larry asked—almost casually. But Sarah wasn't fooled. Larry asked nothing casually.

'We go back a bit,' she told him. 'There was a relationship.'

'Right.' Larry's expression cleared. He'd noticed and he'd needed an explanation. He had one now that satisfied him and he'd take it no further.

'Can you work with the man?'

'I already have. It's fine. Just don't expect us to like each other.'

'I won't do that.' Larry's eyebrows rose. Well, well, his expression said. Dr Rose with a love-life?

Yeah, fat chance, Sarah thought grimly as he disappeared in search of Alistair. Dr Rose with a love-life?

Dr Rose with nothing.

Feeling closer than ever to breaking point, she made her way back to the doctor's quarters and spent an hour making a casserole from Max's offerings. It didn't help her aching heart, but at least... Well, cooking was comfort. Cooking was something she turned to in moments of absolute bleakness.

Like now.

Alistair walked in as she was spooning the casserole onto a plate. Not that she felt like eating. It was the cooking that was important.

'Help yourself,' she told him, and sat and started to eat. Or sat and started to toy with the idea of eating.

He cast her an oddly questioning look, but she wasn't giving any answers. Finally, without comment, he helped himself to a plateful of casserole and sat down with her. He took a forkful and paused.

'Mrs Granson didn't make this.'

'You'd make a fine detective.'

'You made it?'

'Well done. Great deduction.' She wasn't looking at him. She was concentrating fiercely on her food. 'Did Howard give any information?'

He sighed. And moved on. It was the only thing to do. 'No.' He shook his head. 'Larry's pretty sure he knows little himself. Larry showed him the three passports and he said he hadn't a clue how they got there. He's still in a fair amount of pain, and he retreated into feigned sleep, but he said enough for us to realise he's no brain. He'll have been used. He provides a base, and food for people as they come through, but he asks no questions and is told little.'

'You don't think he knows their nationality?'

'I suspect he hasn't even heard of any countries smaller than the United States. He's a serious no-brainer.'

She winced. Another avenue blocked.

More pain, she thought. Her feeling of helplessness was intensifying by the minute—and this man's presence on the other side of the table didn't help at all.

There was a deathly silence, broken only by the sound of Flotsam scratching a flea under the table. It was almost unbearable, Sarah thought. Unbearable…

'Sarah?'

'What?'

'What I said to you in Theatre,' he said at last. 'Putting your actions in the same context as what Barry did to Amal. It was unforgivable.'

More silence. Flotsam's leg thumped the floor in a steady rhythm. He was really enjoying his scratch. Sarah stirred her casserole a bit. It was chicken in an orange sauce with Asian vegetables. Max had done her proud, delving into the depths of his cold store for things he kept for his favourite customers and insisting she take them all. But she couldn't face it. She might just as well be sitting before one of Mrs Granson's offerings.

What was she supposed to say to this man? she wondered. What? There was nothing.

It seemed he knew he had to speak again.

'I was appalled,' he said at last. 'Shocked. Sick at heart. I wanted to lash out and you were there.'

'So you lashed out at me?'

'Yes. Unforgivably. I'm sorry.'

'But you've wanted to lash out at me for six years.'

There was a further silence. It was becoming a habit. Some more casserole stirring. Finally Alistair put down his fork and sighed. He looked up and met her gaze straight on, unflinching.

'That's right,' he told her. 'I have. Of course I have. And you're right in that my anger with you is behind a lot of my tension now. Grant was my twin. I don't know whether you can understand it, but twinship…it's as if you're half of a whole—and when it's ripped away…'

She swallowed and stared at her plate. Half of a whole? Was that how Grant had seen his own twinship? She didn't think so.

'You didn't get on,' she said bleakly.

'No,' he admitted. 'We didn't. We were different people. But that didn't stop me being Grant's twin brother. I'm sure he felt the same. We had our differences, but we would have defended each other to the death.'

Would they? Sarah stared across the table at Alistair and thought, Yes, she could see that in this man. But in his twin?

As he said, they were very different people.

'I had no right to throw it at you this afternoon,' he said heavily. 'Sarah, you've changed. I know you have. I can't get past my anger at Grant's death—I never will—but it did happen six years ago, and I'm starting to realise that you've paid a price, too. You're a different person to the one you were then.'

'Gee, thanks.' She'd been listening with a certain amount of sympathy, but at this her anger surged again. She'd changed, had she? Learned remorse? Learned not to be such a bad little girl that she'd drive a car when she was drugged? That was so good of him. To concede that...

'Hear me out.' He was watching her. It was obvious that he saw her anger, but she could see that he didn't understand. 'All I wanted to say was that whatever's changed in you, Sarah, keep it. With Amal this afternoon you were a caring and compassionate human being—'

'As opposed to what?' she said dangerously. 'As opposed to the drug addict of six years ago?'

His face shuttered and she could see him recoil. 'I'm sorry. I shouldn't have brought it up.'

'You did bring it up,' she managed. 'And how do you think it makes me feel? To be put in the same category as Barry?'

'I didn't mean—'

'You did mean.' She ate a few mouthfuls of her casserole, heaven knew how. The lovely food was threatening to choke her. Finally she pushed her plate back and rose.

'Grant had been drinking,' she said conversationally, and Alistair met her gaze head-on.

'I know,' he conceded. 'Of course I know. So he holds a share of responsibility. Grant got into the car with you when you were on drugs. You don't think I blame him at all? Of course I do. He was stupid and reckless, and I'm not so blinded by loving my twin that I can't accept his stupidity. But you were behind the wheel.'

She could break this now, she thought. She could smash his memories of his beloved brother.

But were those memories all she'd thought they were? What had he said? That Grant had been stupid and reckless. Yes. Yes, he had. And more.

But Alistair still loved him. Could she destroy that? She'd come so far down this road. How could she back out now?

She couldn't. She found now that she didn't even want to. She'd carried this with her for so long that to destroy it... She glanced across at the photograph on the sideboard—Grant laughing and Alistair smiling down at him.

No. She couldn't, and she didn't wish to. Not now. Never.

'I'm going for a walk,' she told him. 'I've eaten enough. I've listened to enough.'

'I've apologised.'

'Yes, and I'm very glad you did. It was incredibly noble.'

'You lost your fiancé, too,' he said, looking up at her with eyes that were intent and searching. 'You loved Grant, too.'

Had she?

'Yeah.'

'Sarah…'

'Leave it.' She bit her lip and carried her plate to the sink. 'Leave the dishes. I'll do them when I come back. I need to go.'

Flotsam came with her. The little dog had decided Sarah was a fun person to be with. He attached himself to her heels and was the only comfort available to her.

The night was still and warm. Sarah walked slowly down the track from the hospital leading to the beach behind.

The tide was out. Miles out. She could barely see the glimmer of surf in the distance. The beach was a vast expanse of wet sand, shimmering golden in the moonlight. Waders—herons, cranes, sandpipers—were paddling in the wet sand, searching for food.

Flotsam made a half-hearted attempt to chase, but she clicked him back to her side. He came obediently and sat beside her as she hugged her knees and looked out into the lonely distance.

'I should never have started this,' she whispered, and Flotsam gave an anxious wuffle and huddled close.

Maybe I should get myself a dog. That was a good thought. It brought a faint smile to her face. She could do it. She could move from her hospital apartment into a bigger place, get herself a yard…

I'm away for most of the day. What sort of life is that for a dog?

No life at all. Her glimmer of pleasure faded.

What am I thinking about? She gave herself a mental swipe—or tried to give herself a mental swipe. She didn't really need it, she decided. She felt pretty battered already.

But it's nothing to what's happening here, she told herself, and she turned so she was looking out at the crags and cliffs along the coastline.

Somewhere out there was a woman and a child, hiding in terror. They'd be waiting desperately for Amal to come back to them, and Amal was fighting for his life in a Cairns hospital. He was probably being operated on right now.

'What can I do to help?' she asked Flotsam, but there was no answer. She felt so…futile. There was nothing. She couldn't search at night—no one could. Tomorrow there'd be a squad of highly trained professionals trawling the hills. Maybe if Amal pulled through they could at least find out his nationality. Then maybe they could pull in translators—people who could call out in the woman's own language. Reassure her…

Oh, sure. As if she'd accept reassurance from the people who shot her husband.

'Can I join you?'

She jumped a foot. Flotsam gave a yelp of excitement and whirled to face his master. Alistair was six feet away.

'Stupid dog,' Sarah managed, thoroughly flustered. 'Great watch dog you'd make. You're supposed to bark.'

'He's barking.'

'When my attacker is right on me.'

'Um…your attacker is the dog's owner,' Alistair said mildly. 'Plus, I'm not exactly intent on rape or pillage.'

'Yeah, but you might have been.'

'You can be very sure I'm not.'

She hugged her knees even harder. Of course. Rape? She

had to be kidding? He wouldn't touch her. She was Grant's
fiancé.

And why would she even want him to? He'd kissed her
once, out of anger and frustration, and there was no way in
the wild world she wanted him to do it again.

Was there?

Where were her thoughts going? All over the place. She
felt as if she was splintering, disintegrating into sharp shards
that hurt.

'I came down here for some peace,' she told him, and he
nodded and sat down on the sand beside her. Obviously her
definition of peace wasn't his.

'You're worried about these people?'

'Of course I'm worried about these people.' She flashed
him a glance that was pure fury. He still thought of her as a
careless, stupid...criminal.

The knowledge cut like a knife.

'There's nothing we can do,' he said heavily, and she nodded, forcing herself to think about problems that weren't hers.

'I can't think of a thing,' she managed. 'They must be
securely hidden by now. And if she's terrified when Amal
doesn't return...'

'She'll have to come out.'

'There's a gun,' she said inconsequentially, and he stared.

'A gun?'

'The pilot was wearing a holster,' she told him. 'It was
empty. In my experience when people wear holsters there's
usually a gun in the vicinity. We all know that. That's why
Barry searched. But there's more than that. The smear of
blood on the seat beside the pilot doesn't belong to him. It's
AB. The pilot is O. So someone—a bleeding someone—
checked the pilot before we reached the plane. Discovered he
was dead. I'm deducing that whoever it was removed the
gun.'

Alistair stared. 'You didn't tell me that.'

'I told Larry.'

'Does Barry know?'

'I'd have been a fool to tell Barry,' she said wearily. 'At least this way he yelled three times before he shot. If he'd known for sure that he had a gun, rather than just suspected it, he might not have given him even that courtesy.'

Alistair sat and thought about it. The silence between them had changed. There was still the tension of anger, but overriding it was the thought of the unknown. A terrified, hurt group of people huddling somewhere in the hills. With a dreadfully wounded child.

'What would you do?' Sarah asked, almost conversationally. 'Let's assume your child is desperately ill. Mortally ill. Your husband goes for help and leaves you hidden. He doesn't return. Two days. Three days. Maybe the child dies. You're bereft in a strange country. Everything you have is gone. And you have a gun.'

'You're imagining things,' Alistair said strongly. He knew where she was headed and the thought was dreadful. 'Anyway…' He hesitated. 'The badly wounded one might be the mother.'

'Would that make it better?'

'No, but…'

'It's not, though,' she told him. 'The father's blood group is O. Most of the blood in the back of the plane is A. There's also a smaller amount of AB, and there's also the blood in the cockpit. An O father and an AB mother can have an A child. An O father and an A mother can't have an AB child.'

'There are assumptions all over the place there,' he said slowly, and she nodded.

'There are. But assumptions are what I do. Acting on scientific evidence, I best-guess and hypothesise. I try and keep an open mind for as long as I can, but when people are depending on me for answers sometimes I just have to guess. I always state absolutely that it's a guess, but it's still a guess, for all that.'

'So what have you guessed?' he asked, and she flinched.

'You sound…sardonic. As far as I know I don't have to answer to you.'

'No.' He was silent for a moment, and then added in a different tone, 'No, you don't. I'm sorry. I didn't mean to sound sardonic. I would like to know what you've guessed.'

She stared out to sea for a long moment, as if she was considering whether to speak or not. In truth she wasn't being difficult. She just needed time to adjust—to adjust to the feel of him sitting beside her. The sensation of the night.

The sensation of him.

But finally she spoke, forcing her mind to track again through what it had tracked over and over again over the last days. What she'd expounded to Larry as the most probable course of events.

'We have a smuggling ring,' she told him. 'A team set up to take advantage of desperate people who, for whatever reason, can't use or don't know about the normal refugee channels. Amal looks Middle Eastern, and we know how much unrest is over there. So for some reason he was in serious trouble. He needed to get his family out of the country fast. He looks as if he's been well dressed, his hands are those of a professional, rather than a manual worker, and his clothes aren't cheap. So let's say he had money.'

'Assumptions.'

'Do you want to hear this or do you want to leave me to my beach? Alone.'

'I'm sorry.' He held his hands up, placating. Asking her to proceed.

'Fine,' she snapped. She tugged Flotsam to her and hugged him. She was wearing shorts and T-shirt; the night wind was soft and warm and she wasn't cold, but still she shivered. She had need of Flotsam.

'Okay,' she continued finally. 'Our people paid through the nose to be taken out of the country—say to some nice safe country like Australia. They were kept well clear of normal channels of transport. Normal refugee channels. They were taken overland, or by cheap flights to Asia, then onward by boat and landed on a remote beach somewhere up north. Then our pilot picked them up, only he was a fool, with a plan for more easy cash, and he died. They crashed.'

'I've figured this out—'

'Bear with me,' she snapped. 'I'm thinking out loud, and it helps if I do the whole scenario. So they crashed. The child was badly wounded—a lot of blood. The mother was slightly wounded.'

'You don't know—'

'Wait.' She glowered. 'As I said, it's assumption. But we have a dreadfully wounded child, a slightly wounded mother, and a father who's okay. He'd have got them all out of the plane. His attention would have been on the child. But what was his next action?'

'Check the pilot?'

'Yeah. But the kid needed him. His wife maybe had a bleeding hand—something—not too much. So he'd have told her to check. She climbed up, leaving blood. She saw that the pilot was dead. And she saw the gun. She was in the middle of nowhere. Scared silly. Terrified. Of course she'd have taken the gun.'

'So why didn't he bring it?' Alistair said slowly. 'When he came to rob the store?'

'Two reasons I can think of,' Sarah said. 'Either he doesn't know she has it, or he's left it with her. To defend herself. And neither scenario appeals. What we're left with is a terrified, desperate woman with a gun.'

'Hell,' Alistair said softly, and Sarah nodded.

'It is. For her it must be.'

'So what do we do?'

'Hope Amal pulls through,' Sarah said. 'Hope he can tell the police in Cairns where he comes from so we can at least call out in the woman's own language. Larry agrees that we need to remove every uniform and every gun or anything that can be remotely taken for a gun at a distance from searchers.

If she thinks anyone's armed it'll make things worse. We'll try and figure out through their names where they come from—there are people trying to do that now. As for the rest…' She hugged Flotsam some more. 'Nothing,' she said bitterly. 'Until the searchers go out tomorrow morning… nothing.'

'You really care, don't you?'

'What do you think?'

There was a long, long silence. Sarah dug her toes into the sun-warmed sand. The night was closing in on them now—the moon was full over the sea and the shimmer of its light over the far-off waves made this place look lovely. An enticing land.

But it wasn't, Sarah thought. It was deceiving. In a couple of hours the tide would sweep in and this would be underwater. There was no shelter. The mangrove swamps held crocodiles; there was no food; every scratch would fester in this warm, muggy climate.

Somewhere…

'Sarah?' Alistair said, so softly that at first she thought she'd imagined it. But she looked up and he was watching her, his eyes gravely questioning.

'Yes?'

'I wanted to ask you…' He hesitated, as though not sure how to begin. Or even if he wanted to begin.

What was he going to ask? Sarah thought, half fearful.

And she was right to be fearful. His question, when it came, was right out of left field. He put a hand down and his finger traced the deep and jagged scar running the length of her left leg. 'Sarah, how did you get this scar?'

He shouldn't have asked. Long ago he'd had an odd and occasionally silly great-aunt who'd drummed in her Rules To Live By. 'Don't ask questions, boy. You might get answers you don't like, and then where would you be, hey?'

That was how he felt now. But the question had been growing. The deep sense of unease. The feeling…

No. He wasn't going to begin to acknowledge the feeling he had. The foreboding. He couldn't. Until he heard the answer.

But he knew that he was right the moment he looked up from tracing the scar and saw her eyes. He saw the fear.

'In the accident,' she said, so softly that he had to lean forward to make sure he heard it.

'In the accident—when Grant died?'

'Yes.'

'But…' He was motionless. It was as if the whole world was holding its breath. He should shut up, he thought. He should back out right now. This was Grant they were talking about. It was as if he had to make a choice right now—Grant or Sarah.

Grant was his twin.

But Grant was dead. Six years dead. And Sarah was alive, living with consequences he could hardly bear to think about.

'This is a jagged tear to the outside of your left leg,' he said slowly, as if each word was torn from him. 'And the only side of the car that was damaged was the passenger side.'

'Well, then.' She swallowed and tried to rise. His hand stopped her.

'Sarah…'

'Don't ask, Alistair,' she begged. 'Grant's your twin. You love him. Don't ask.'

But he didn't have to ask. He already knew the answer.

'Grant was driving,' he whispered. 'My God…Grant was driving. But how…? How…? Did you agree to take the blame?' And then, as she stayed silent, he thought back. 'You had concussion. I remember. When Grant rang he said you had concussion and lacerations. That'd fit if you were in the passenger side. But he told me that you were driving.'

'We hit a tree,' Sarah told him. 'When the police arrived Grant had hauled me out of the car.'

'That's what he told them?'

'I assume. I was unconscious.'

'He'd been drinking.' Alistair swallowed. All the old anger came flooding back. The fury. The waste of it. The sheer bloody waste. And this girl…

'He'd have been over the legal alcohol limit. To save losing his licence he dragged you out and he blamed you. Is that right, Sarah? Is that right?'

Sarah flinched. It had never been said. It had never been faced. And now it was harder to admit than she'd thought possible.

'It's right,' she whispered. 'I never had the chance to ask him—to confront him—but it must have been right. To lose his driver's licence…to have it in the newspapers that he'd crashed while driving under the influence… You know how much he'd have hated it. But me… I had sedatives in my bloodstream, but there's no law against that. Rumours were that I'd taken all sorts of illegal drugs, but there was nothing illegal about it. Grant knew that. He knew that if he said I was driving I wouldn't be charged.'

'But…he was dying.'

'He didn't think there was anything wrong with him.' Sarah gave a bitter laugh. 'You know that. He mustn't have been wearing his seat belt. Not even that. He was drunk; he wasn't wearing his seat belt; and he thought he'd walked away from the wreck without any injury.'

'And you let him… You let him accuse you.'

'I had concussion,' Sarah said. 'I lost a lot of blood. I was taken to hospital, and as soon as I came round they gave me an anaesthetic and stitched my leg. It was a big job, so they used a general anaesthetic. I was hazy—in and out of consciousness for almost a day. And when I surfaced they told me Grant was dead. Dead. That was it. No one interviewed me. No one asked me questions. I didn't have to tell anyone what had happened because Grant had made a full statement to the police naming me as the driver. No one even asked me to explain the traces of sedative they found in my blood-stream.'

Alistair sat, silent. Trying to absorb it. He scarcely could. But it fitted. Dreadful as it was, it fitted.

But Sarah... To wake like that. What must it have been like, regaining consciousness? Waking? Being told Grant was dead?

Being told that Grant had stated that it was all her fault.

'They believed it when you agreed you were the driver?' Alistair whispered, and Sarah gave a bitter laugh.

'No. I told you. They didn't have to believe me. Not one person has ever asked me whether I was driving. No one. They believed Grant. How much easier to believe than to ask questions? The coroner's verdict was that the car had spun out when it hit ice. An accident. No need for questions.'

'But—'

'Why do you think I decided to be a forensic pathologist?' she demanded, her voice laced with the bitterness of years. 'When the people at work shunned me because of what I'd done and I decided to change careers it was the obvious choice. I figured if I could stop one person going through what I'd gone through it'd be worthwhile. Join the police force, study forensic medicine, save the world.' She tried to smile, but there was an obvious and dreadful pain behind the smile. A pain he couldn't believe he'd missed until now.

'They were all so stupid,' she whispered. 'They believed. And what was I to do?'

'You could have told the truth.'

'Right.'

'You could have.'

'Could I? Could I really? Could I have told the world that not only was Grant dead but he was a liar? Could I have told your parents that? Shattered their world still more? Could I have told you? I knew how unwell your father was—he was the nicest man. And you...'

Her voice faded almost to nothing, but then she regrouped—just a little. 'How would you have felt?' she asked, 'Not only was your brother dead, but he'd been driving drunk and in the few minutes when he should have been trying to stop my leg from bleeding he'd carted me around to the other side of the car and made it seem as if I was the driver. Afterwards I went to see the car, where it lay in the wrecker's yard. If you knew what you were looking for it was so obvious. Do you know, he even wiped my blood from the passenger door? The doctors told me I almost died through blood loss. I lay bleeding while he covered his traces. But then he paid the ultimate price. He died.'

Alistair thought it through, and thought some more. It didn't help. His head felt as if it was close to bursting. Whichever way he looked at it he felt sick. Unbearably ill.

He'd seen the car. He hadn't looked. He hadn't asked questions. And Sarah had paid the price.

'You've carried this all this time.'

'I had no choice. Grant gave me this legacy.'

'But you…' He stared at her in the moonlight, trying to see… Trying to see what? He didn't know. 'You were on drugs…'

Anger flared then. Real and dreadful. 'Does that make it easier to bear? Your brother blamed me but, hey, it's okay, she's just a hophead?'

'No, but—'

'You want to know the truth about that, too?'

He didn't. But he must. 'Yes.'

'It was because of my mother,' she told him.

She stood then, pushing herself up, walking away and looking out to sea—as if she couldn't bear to face him.

'I've already told you my mother was an alcoholic,' she said. 'She never got over my father walking out on her, and that happened before I was born. She suffered from depression, exacerbated by the alcohol. She was in and out of nursing homes from the time I was tiny—on uppers, downers, the works. She and I hadn't had any real relationship for years, though I tried. Heaven knows I tried. Anyway, that night she rang me, when I was working at the hospital, and said I had to come around to her apartment. She had a surprise for me. Something she wanted me to share with my father. She was insistent. I had to come. God help me, she even sounded excited.'

'And?' Alistair found he was holding his breath, and he didn't know how long he'd been holding it. For ten minutes? Longer. An eternity. He took a long, searing breath and tried to concentrate.

'She'd suicided,' Sarah said flatly. 'Of course she had. Some things are inevitable. It was her last sick joke on the world. On me. On life. She'd planned it so I'd find her and I had to cut her down. She thought…she'd have thought that by hurting me she'd somehow hurt my father. The sick thing is that he couldn't have cared less.'

'Oh, Sarah…'

'I called the police, the undertaker—everyone,' she said. 'A doctor arrived at some stage. I was… Well, I was in a mess. Despite everything, I still loved her. The doctor who came knew Grant, and he knew who I was. He thought I was still… Well, he knew about our relationship. So he called him and Grant came.' She gave a shrug of her shoulders, eloquently expressive in the moonlight. 'That sort of thing— drama, suicide, me being distraught—would have appealed to Grant. I knew him pretty well by then. Too well. Because of my father, the suicide would hit the headlines, and Grant knew that. It was what he most liked about me. My famous father. It had taken me a while to see, but I knew it then, and I never should have let him be called. If the paparazzi were nearby then Grant would relish it. Only there weren't any paparazzi. My mother had got past the stage where the press were interested.'

Alistair was scarcely breathing. At the time of Grant's death he hadn't seen either of them for a couple of months, but what she was saying made sense. Every time Grant had talked about Sarah the name of her famous father had come up.

Would Grant have loved Sarah if her father wasn't famous? He couldn't ask. But he knew the answer.

'Couldn't your father come?' he asked her, and watched as she shook her head, bleakness intensifying.

'What do you think? He was in Switzerland—with another of his women. Being famous. Sure, there'd be paparazzi where my father was, but the suicide of an elderly, drunk ex-wife could be hushed up. I told Grant that was what I wanted—that things be kept quiet—and he had to agree.'

'I see.'

'Do you?' she asked bleakly. 'Do you? Because that's how it happened. He'd been drinking, and I was too upset to think straight. He came into my mother's apartment and he acted the real doctor. Specialist in charge. Which, of course, he was. "I'll take charge," he told everyone. He gave me sedatives and I didn't argue. "I'll take you home," he said, and that was the last thing I remember.'

'Why did I know nothing of this?' Alistair felt sick. To say he was appalled… There was no way he could begin to describe how he felt. His world was shifting under his feet. Grant. Grant had done this—to Sarah. 'Why did I know nothing about what happened to your mother?'

'You didn't ask,' Sarah told him, weary now beyond belief. 'I told you. Nobody asked. No one came near me. I made my decision to wear Grant's blame because I didn't think your parents could bear it if I didn't. I wore it. And you all just accepted it. Because, of course, you loved Grant. Everyone loved Grant. God help me, for a short, short time I thought I did, too. But I've paid for that loving. It's a long time since I loved him, but everyone else still does.'

There was an end to it. Her voice faded to nothing. Her world seemed to fade to nothing. Or maybe it had faded a long time ago.

Sarah stood looking out to sea for a long, long time, while Alistair stayed silent behind her.

There was nothing to be said. Nothing to say. She'd made her decision six years ago. If she'd had a choice that decision would have been held for life. But now…

Grant was his twin. What she'd just done to Alistair was inexcusable. But he'd asked. He'd probed as no one else ever had.

'I'm going back to the house,' she said at last, and she walked away without looking back.

Not even Flotsam followed her.

CHAPTER NINE

IT WAS almost two in the morning before he came to her.

She'd lain in the dark, staring at the moonlit ceiling, her mind almost blank. She'd gone past thinking.

Once upon a time she'd made a conscious decision not to hurt these people. She remembered the time she'd spent on Grant's family farm, so long ago. Grant had take her there for Christmas. Until then her relationship with Grant had been light, and she'd had little intention of taking it further. But when he'd discovered she had nowhere to go for Christmas—her dysfunctional family hadn't celebrated Christmas for years—he'd insisted that she come.

'You'll be bored to snores,' he'd told her. 'Mum and Dad are simple farmers and Alistair's not much better—a country doctor, for heaven's sake. But they do a good Christmas dinner and you'll keep me entertained.'

She hadn't kept Grant entertained. How could she have? He'd been bored with the farm—with his family—but whereas Grant had been bored, the farm had entranced Sarah. The family had entranced her. The warmth of Grant's parents, the laughter, the love, the ease with which they accepted each other. Alistair had been there the whole time. They had been raking hay, and she remembered that summer harvest and Christmas time as being one of the happiest of her life.

Grant had come and gone—he'd made two trips back to the city while she'd been there—but she'd stayed on. She'd relished every minute of her stay and afterwards, when Grant had asked her to marry him, she'd said yes.

Of course she'd said yes. For Sarah, who'd never known such a family, the thought had been irresistible. She'd loved them. She could never have hurt them.

She'd hurt Alistair now. Hurt him beyond bearing.

She stared at the ceiling some more and tried to get her thoughts to focus. They wouldn't, and when the door opened just a crack she almost welcomed it.

'Sarah? Are you asleep?'

'What do you think?' She pushed herself up on the pillows and swiped her hair behind her ears. Her cheeks were wet, she noticed with an almost dispassionate interest. Had she been crying?

The door was wide then. Alistair stood there, as if uncertain. He was still in his day gear—maybe he hadn't been to bed.

'I've been walking.'

'That's a stupid thing to do,' she told him. 'The night's for sleeping.'

'So I'm stupid. What else is new?'

'Go to bed, Alistair,' she told him.

But he wasn't listening. He was a dark shadow in the doorway. Motionless. Almost formless.

'Do you know,' he said softly, as if he hadn't heard her. 'If Grant hadn't died then I wouldn't have believed him. I wouldn't have accepted his word that the accident was your fault. Believe it or not, I'd stopped believing Grant a long time before he died. And I shouldn't have believed him even then. I saw the car. The wrecker rang and said there were things left in the trunk. I went round to collect them and I saw the thing. But I was so shocked. I saw the passenger side was damaged and I saw the driver's side was fine. But Grant was dead. My father had collapsed. My head didn't do the sums. My head didn't even think about doing the sums.'

'Go to bed, Alistair,' she said again. 'Don't do this to yourself. I shouldn't have told you. I'm sorry.'

'No,' he told her, and then more forcibly, 'No!' He walked forward, the formless shadow became the man, and before she knew what he was about he'd taken her shoulders in his hands, gripping hard. She could feel his anger now, as well as hear it.

'Don't you dare be sorry,' he told her. 'Don't you think about it for a minute longer. You didn't do this to me. Grant did this. He lied and he cheated and he risked your life. This was Grant's doing and I can't help that you loved him. You have to see… Sarah, you have to see that he's not worth protecting. He's dead, Sarah. He's gone. Don't you dare apologise to me for what he did to you.'

She didn't know what to say. His hands shifted to grip her hands. Urgent with the need to convince. His words echoed around her head.

And inside her she felt a knot unfasten. Loosen. Release. It was a knot of pain so great and so hard that she could hardly believe it was going. It was as if half of her was being torn away.

And, confusingly, she felt naked without it—exposed. For so long she'd lived with this thing.

'Alistair…'

'You let my parents die thinking ill of you,' he said, and the fury was still there. 'I can't bear it.'

'Your parents—'

'My parents loved you. You stayed with us a week and in that week you became part of our lives. And then…nothing. You and Grant didn't go near them for months. How do you think they felt? Thinking that they'd misjudged you so badly? Thinking that you'd killed Grant?'

'I—'

But he hadn't finished. 'They hated it. They'd hoped, like I had, that at last Grant had found himself something beautiful, something worthwhile, someone worth loving. And he had. We all had. And you gave us that gift. The gift of thinking Grant wasn't as worthless as we'd feared.'

'He wasn't—'

'He was.' His grip tightened. 'I can't bear it,' he said again, in a voice that was thick with anger—and more. Thick with…passion? 'I can't bear that you did this thing to yourself. I can't bear that you protected him.' And then, more softly, 'I can't bear it that you loved him.'

He couldn't bear it? How could *she*? 'Leave it,' she whispered.

'How can I leave it?'

'It's over,' she said, her voice flat and dead. Trying to kill something, she was starting to learn, was capable of hurting even more than the pain she felt for Grant.

'How can it be over?' he demanded. 'How can it be over when I feel for you as I feel? When I feel for you like this?'

Like…?

But she didn't have to ask like what. It was a stupid question, only half formed in her mind and never voiced.

She knew what he felt. Because she felt it, too.

As if they were two halves of a whole.

This man…

She remembered the first time she'd seen him, walking into the ward at the children's hospital. The next minute he'd been down on the floor, being a crab with her and with the children who'd so desperately needed to laugh. Losing his dignity as Grant never, ever would have.

She'd fallen in love right there. She hadn't realised it. She'd thought it was an extension of what she'd felt for Grant.

Grant. She had loved him. She'd loved his family.

She couldn't have his family. She'd have Grant.

No. She couldn't have Alistair. She'd have Grant.

How long ago had she realised that it was love for Alistair that was keeping her tied to Grant? How long before she'd accepted the truth and given Grant back his ring?

Not very long, she thought bleakly. She'd broken off the engagement well before that awful night, but he had still been interested, still persistent, and *in extremis,* when she'd desperately needed someone, he'd been there.

But it was Alistair she'd wanted. Alistair—who'd been going out with someone else, who didn't have a clue how she felt…

This man.

This man who was sitting before her in the moonlight. He was gripping her hands so tightly they hurt. He was so close…

He was pulling her into his arms where she belonged…

She was so lovely. She was everything he wanted in a woman. She was Sarah.

Sarah.

She was melting into his arms. Her face was turning up to his. Her lips were against his and he could feel the soft sweetness of her. He could taste the loveliness of her.

Sarah.

His senses shut down. Everything shut down.

There was only Sarah.

How long could the moment last? How far could they go? Alistair had no idea, but when it ended it was as if they both expected it. This joy wasn't rightfully theirs. It was unbelievable. Unattainable.

This woman had loved Grant. His brother.

She had no place with him.

So when the sound of the phone jarred in the silence it was as if both expected it, and when they pulled away he could see that she had known it would happen.

There was no joy in her eyes. No love. Instead her face looked bruised. Frightened. She'd been weeping, he thought, and he swore and put a finger up to trace the path of a teardrop down her cheek.

'Sarah, don't. I can't bear it. I didn't mean to make you cry.'

'You didn't. You couldn't…' She was almost incoherent.

The phone was ringing still, but they ignored it. Some things were too important even for the imperatives of medicine to interrupt.

'I love you,' he whispered, but he knew at once that it was

a mistake. He felt the sudden rigidity of her body. He felt the shock wave running through her slight frame and he knew there was no joy here this night.

'No.'

'Yes.'

'Grant,' she said, then faltered, and the tension in her body was suddenly matched by his. 'I can't… Because of Grant… Don't say you love me, Alistair. I was your twin's fiancée and this night I've shocked you to the core. You don't know what you're saying. You feel sorry for me, Alistair, and I can't get past that. Not yet. Not now. Do you think I'd let you make love with me now—when there's this between us?'

'No, but—'

'I knew how it'd be,' she said bleakly. 'I desperately didn't want to tell you. I didn't want to give you this guilt.'

'I'm not wearing guilt.'

'You're saying if this hadn't happened you'd be kissing me? This isn't love, Alistair. This is shock. Passion of anger and pain and distress.' Then, as he hesitated, she pulled away from him completely. 'Answer the phone, Alistair,' she whispered. 'You need to.'

'I don't want—'

'You don't know what you want and neither do I. Answer the phone.'

He stared at her, balked. Frustrated. Her face had shuttered. Her eyes were blank and weary.

'It's too late,' she said, turning away from him. 'Or too early. It's almost dawn. And I can't face you. Not yet. Not now. I can't take this forward. Just go and answer the phone, Alistair, and leave me be.'

How could he leave her? He couldn't. But of course, as always, there were medical imperatives. Howard was awake and writhing with pain. One of the stones must be pushing through. He needed to increase the morphine dose and give the man some reassurance that he wasn't dying.

He had to go. Like it or not.

'We'll leave it for now, but we can't leave this for ever,' he told her.

He'd answered the phone set up in the hall so he was standing in her doorway again, with Sarah a shadow silhouetted against the moonlight in the window.

'We'll leave it till morning,' she whispered, almost grateful 'Meanwhile…go and see to Howard. Let me think.'

It wasn't only pain and fear of his illness keeping Howard awake. Alistair increased his morphine dose, but before he could leave the man gripped his arm and started pleading.

'I'm not responsible. I dunno who all these people are.'

Alistair nodded. He wanted to go back to Sarah. He desperately wanted to get back to Sarah. There was so much left unsaid.

But there were other imperatives. Deadly imperatives. He knew that. If staying here could get them information…

'You've had lots of people through the property?'

'Heaps,' Howard told him. He'd obviously been lying in the dark, in pain, and had decided the only way through this was to be helpful. 'But I never knew who any of them were. Most from those places with funny names like Iran and Iraq or Kurb… Kurb… Anyway, places like that. They never said anything. The pilots would drop them off, I'd feed them and give them the passports and stuff, show 'em a few videos about living here, and in a few days a truck'd come and fetch them.'

'A truck?'

'They'd go on one of the transporters that take the cattle down south. It was all paid for. The truck drivers didn't know nothing, either. No one did.'

'You know that the pilot died?'

'Yeah, but I didn't know him. He was a newbie. We'd had the same pilot for two years but he got cold feet. The boss said he was sending someone out from Thailand to take over the run.'

'The boss?'

Howard chewed his lip. 'Yeah. The boss. I'm not supposed to know who he is.'

'But you do?'

'I might.'

'Can you contact him?'

'Maybe.' Howard shifted in his bed and winced. 'I'm not supposed to know anything at all. But he came here once to check the place out and…well, I checked his wallet when he was in the shower. I'm no happier to work in the dark than the next man.'

'He's Australian?'

'Yeah. Do you reckon if I fingered him they'd be easier on me?'

'I'm sure they would,' Alistair told him. He was focused now, knowing this could be vital information. His own personal needs—what lay between him and Sarah—had to be put aside for this. It must. 'Do you want me to ask the senior detective to talk to you?'

'What'd you reckon?'

'I reckon it might help. And that has to count for something.'

It might well help. More than anything right now he wanted to go back to Sarah, but he knew enough of human nature to know that Howard was likely to change his mind at any minute. If he clammed up, this opportunity could well be lost.

'I'll phone the detective now,' he told Howard, and Howard nodded.

'You stay, though,' he told Alistair. 'They put words in a man's mouth, these coppers. You stay with us while he's here or I'm saying nothing.'

Alistair nodded. It meant he couldn't go back to Sarah. It meant he might be stuck here for an hour.

Maybe it was just as well.

*   *   *

How could she think?

Sarah couldn't. She lay and stared at the ceiling until the first glimmers of dawn lit the room. Four a.m. Four-thirty. Enough. Alistair wasn't returning and she was going crazy.

She needed a walk. She needed to do anything but lie here and go crazy. Silently she rose and dressed, hauling on jeans and sweatshirt and trainers. Then she walked out into the dawn, closing the door firmly on Flotsam as he tried to follow.

'No, boy. Not this morning. I need my own company.'

And how lonely was that?

She couldn't answer her question. There was so much happening. So much…

She walked. She walked for miles along the sea-washed beach. But it didn't help. Nothing helped, and finally she turned. She knew she had to return to the house. To Alistair.

To sort out for ever what lay between them.

To somehow forge a way forward.

Who was she kidding? There was no way forward.

She was alone for ever.

Dolphin Creek's tiny police station was on the main street. Barry usually slept out on the veranda—it was cooler that way—and right now he appreciated it. Right now he needed as much cooling as he could get.

He was suspended. Suspended pending investigation.

He knew what that meant. The end of his police career.

But why? For the life of him he couldn't appreciate why everyone was so worried about the low-life criminal element he dealt with. And he was a good cop. He knew he was. Much better than the mealy-mouthed, psychology-trained cadets coming into the force these days.

He didn't like the direction the force was taking. Maybe it was time he moved on.

But he had no wish to move on. Despite the hassles he'd had over the last couple of years, despite the implied demotion in being sent to Dolphin Creek, he liked being a policeman. He liked wearing a gun on his hip and having people treat him with the respect he deserved. He liked neatness and order, and he liked people paying the penalty if they flouted that sense of order.

So what was happening to him right now made no sense at all to the aggrieved police officer. He'd shot an illegal refugee—a criminal. A person of no worth at all. And now he was going to lose his career because of it.

His anger was building all through the night. He lay awake and stared out at the deserted street and thought about it. And fumed. And somewhere in the time between darkness and dawn the fine line between reason and irrational fury was crossed.

That was how he was when he saw the woman. She was a ragged figure, carting what looked like the doc's big medical bag down the street, darting from shadow to shadow.

He did nothing. Who gave a toss? he thought sourly. He could bring her in. That'd please them. But then, why should he lift a finger to help? Damn them all. They could go chase their tails.

He was suspended.

Only then he saw her go past again, a stooped figure pushing Florence Trotman's wheelbarrow. She was still darting from shadow to shadow, pushing the barrow before her.

He watched for a while and saw her for a third time. This time her barrow was loaded, not just with the doctor's bag, but also with a pile of things that looked from this distance like basic supplies. Mounds of bottled water. Bread.

Petty pilfering. Why should he care?

She didn't look anything, he thought. Certainly not the hardened criminal he'd thought was probably behind this whole thing. She looked…pathetic. Maybe she was a stooge, expendable, being sent into town to fetch.

Taking her out would achieve nothing. There must be someone behind her.

She was headed north.

Were they hiding north, then? Despite his determination not

to get involved, he couldn't prevent a rousing interest. He lay back on his bunk and tried to figure it out. Who would have thought that they'd hide out north of the town? They must have skirted the town's boundaries, maybe coming close so they could steal.

Where would they hide within wheelbarrow-pushing distance north of the town? The land out there was barren. Empty. There were only the cliffs.

The caves. If they'd come down from the hills looking for supplies then the closest place to hide would be the caves.

Stuff it, he wasn't going to help. He was suspended.

He lay still. But his mind wouldn't cease thinking.

Sarah was quickening her steps as she walked back towards town. She'd come too far. Soon the team would be heading out to the wreck and she needed to go with them.

But still nothing was resolved. The ache in her heart was as dreadful as ever.

No matter. Only work mattered. Work was her salvation. Not this deserted beach. Not this time.

Not Alistair.

Reluctantly she walked on—and then she paused. There was a figure coming down the sand-hills towards her.

For a moment she thought it could be Alistair and she felt a jolt of pure wild hope. Stupid hope.

Was it? She shaded her eyes. The sun had crept over the horizon now, and was a low, golden ball in the morning sky.

Who was it?

Not Alistair. No.

She walked a little further and the figure turned into a woman: a woman dressed in something that might once have been some sort of Eastern European gown but was now ripped and ragged. A bloodstained rag was tied around her wrist. The woman was walking haltingly, staggering a little on the soft sand.

Sarah stopped. Her heart rose almost into her mouth. Dear God…

'Noa?' Her voice was a whisper. She raised it a little. 'Are you Noa?'

The woman didn't respond. She kept walking towards her, each step deliberate, her eyes on Sarah's face. One hand was held behind her back, the other was held out almost in entreaty.

She neared her. Three yards. Two.

Her hand came out from behind her ragged gown. A gun pointed straight at Sarah.

Both women stopped. The gun stayed rock-steady.

'Come with me,' the woman said. 'Come with me now. Your people have killed my husband. Now you save my son or you die.'

CHAPTER TEN

THE interview with Howard took a good hour, but maybe it was worth it. Alistair and Larry had listened to Howard's rambling story. At the end of it they had a formal statement, duly witnessed.

'It'll help,' Larry said in satisfaction as they left the room. He glanced down at the name Howard had given them. 'This is great. I know him. We've been after this guy for years. There's been nothing but suspicions, but now a statement in front of an independent witness… It's fantastic.'

'All we have to do is find these people.'

'Yeah.' Larry nodded. 'We leave at six.' He shrugged. 'It's five o'clock now. Not worth going back to bed.' He gave a wry smile. 'Who needs sleep?'

'Obviously not us,' Alistair agreed as they walked out to the hospital entrance together. He thought of what he intended doing right now, and sleep was way down on the list. In truth, it was so far down he couldn't even see it.

All he could see was Sarah.

But then his thoughts were interrupted. His truck…

Alistair's truck was parked just by the hospital entrance, and the damage was apparent the moment they stepped out through the door. Someone had smashed the rear window. A shower of broken glass covered the ground around it.

Why?

One glance and it was obvious.

Alistair's doctor's bag was gone. All the medical equipment he left permanently ready for emergencies had disappeared.

*   *   *

The cave was located in just about the last place Sarah would have thought of searching. Where anyone would have thought of searching.

For a start, the cave was north of the town, and the plane had been wrecked to the south. It was set in the cliffs back from the beach, a dry and dusty place where nothing grew. There was a cleft in the rocks and Noa waved the gun at Sarah, motioning her through.

'Hurry.'

The woman looked distraught to the point of madness. She was still young—though older than Sarah's twenty-nine years. Her dark hair, braided down her back, was still jet-black, though it was matted with red dust, and the braid had long ago frayed to the point where it was only just recognisable as a plait. Her dark eyes were sunk into a gaunt face, and they were ringed with the telltale shadows of exhaustion.

The hand holding the gun shook with weariness and with fear.

Sarah hadn't spoken to her as they'd walked up the beach towards the cave. The woman seemed tense to the point of breaking. It therefore seemed sensible to simply do as she asked, with no questions.

'Go,' the woman said, and shoved the gun at her. There was no choice. Sarah slid through the cleft in the rock and went.

Behind the cleft was an open stretch of sand, with three walls of sheer cliff face. An overhang gave shade, and the north face sloped upward at an angle that let in the morning sun but was steep enough to stop the wind. As a shelter it was bleak, but it was adequate.

But Sarah wasn't considering her surroundings.

On the ground before her lay a child, and one look made Sarah's heart sink. Ignoring the gun, ignoring the woman, she got down on the ground. This was what she'd most feared.

He was tiny. Tinier than she'd expected. Five, the passport had said, but he looked even younger. Four, maybe?

He lay on a bundle of clothing in the dust, his face pressed hard into the mound of cloth. A tiny, gaunt child, as dark as his mother, his tiny frame almost skeletal.

There was good light. This was more a rock shelter than a proper cave. The morning sun glinted downward through the sloping north face of rock, illuminating the deathly shadowed face of the child lying so still that death was a distinct possibility.

He was so tiny. And so dreadfully hurt. He was wearing bloodstained shorts and a T-shirt. A bandage was wound around his leg—white cloth, roughly torn. Through the cloth was the unmistakable sign of a suppurating wound.

Infection.

It had to be. Sarah thought back to the rough metal container, loose in the cargo hold. It had looked rusty and none too clean.

Regardless of the gun, regardless of the woman, she crouched in the dust in an instant. Her fingers were feeling the child's pulse as she searched his body for more clues to what was happening to him. Somewhere above her the woman was still pointing the gun, but she ignored her. There were no threats needed to make her treat this child.

'He needs help,' she whispered. At least he was still alive, but that was all that could be said. The little one's pulse was thready and weak. He was hot to touch. She could feel the fever in him. Forty? Forty-one?

'Help him, then,' the woman told her, and Sarah sat back on her heels and looked up at her.

'You have good English?'

'Yes.'

'We must get more help than just me,' Sarah said, trying to keep the urgency from her voice. Trying to suppress panic. How long had this infection had to take hold? 'He needs hospital. Doctors.'

'You are a doctor. I heard you say…when you shot my husband.'

Sarah took a deep breath. And another.

'I didn't shoot your husband,' she said, trying to keep her voice even. 'I never would. It was a mistake.'

'My husband tried to get food. You shot him. Now you help us.'

'I can't,' Sarah said, trying to keep the desperation from her voice. 'Your son needs fluids. He needs antibiotics. He needs specialist equipment.'

'I have equipment,' the woman told her. She pointed to a pile near the cliff face. 'I brought it.'

Sarah stared to where she was pointing, recognising immediately what was there. Alistair's bag. And groceries. A pile of stuff heaped into an ancient wheelbarrow.

'My husband is a doctor,' the woman said, in faltering, fearful English. 'He is a good man, but not…maybe not very wise. He said…he said he would not take the gun with him when he went to steal. He just wished to take food. And now he's dead.'

'He's not dead.'

'He's shot. I saw him. I followed, though he told me not to. But I was so afraid. I was so fearful for his life that I left our son for a little. And I was right to be afraid. They took him away. There was so much blood I was almost ill. So much blood. Almost as much as when Azron was injured. So now my son's fate lies in my hands and I will do what I must. I took the gun. I went into town and I found these things. I brought them here and then I saw you, walking alone. The gun will do what my husband cannot. The gun will save my son.'

'Alistair.'

It was Max, dishevelled and out of breath. Larry and Alistair were still staring at the truck when Max pounded into the car park. 'Do you know where—' He stopped, recognising Larry. 'Detective…'

'What's the problem?' The police detective had turned from the smashed car to the storekeeper and his voice was professionally clipped, forcing Max to stop in his tracks and re-group. 'Stop,' Larry ordered. 'Take three deep breaths and then tell us. Slow.'

And Max did. Somehow.

'She broke into the store,' he told them. 'You know I sleep in the room right behind the store? I heard a window smash and she was there, in the doorway, pointing a gun straight at me. A woman. In rags. She looked awful. Scared to death. She made me pack a heap of stuff—water, biscuits, bread—and then she made me carry it all outside. She had a wheel-barrow. A bloody wheelbarrow. It's the one Florence Trotman uses to plant her pansies in every winter. She'd emptied the whole thing out. And, Alistair, she had a heap of your stuff in it. Then she made me go into the outhouse and she barri-caded the door. She said if I tried to break out in less than twenty minutes she'd be standing outside and would shoot to kill. I knew it'd be to give her time to get away but, bugger me, I wasn't taking any chances. Not for a bit of bread and water.'

'Twenty minutes?' Larry snapped, and Max took another couple of deep breaths and looked just a bit sheepish.

'Maybe thirty. Bloody woman. I wasn't going to take any chances, and neither of us were wearing a watch.' And then he shrugged. 'Look, she seemed desperate. After what hap-pened last time I wasn't risking her not getting what she needed.'

'What was she wearing?' Larry asked, and as Max gave a description his face tightened into grim lines. Max's descrip-tion of the woman was graphic, and they could all imagine her desperation. Her fear. Alistair could see why Max had decided to take no chances. This was a description of a woman close to madness.

And she'd had half an hour's start.

'She was pushing the wheelbarrow?' Alistair asked, and Max nodded.

'Yeah.'

'Then we can follow the tracks, surely?'

'I don't like our odds,' Larry told him. 'In this wind?' While they'd been speaking the wind had been strengthening. Sand was swirling along the street, leaving a film over everything it reached. Half an hour… Maybe they could follow it. Maybe not.

Probably not.

'You have no idea which way she went?' Larry asked, and Max shook his head.

'I'll fetch the trackers,' Larry said grimly. 'We'll get everyone on this straight away, fanning out between here and the wreck. Alistair, go and fetch Sarah. I suspect what we have here is a terrified woman who's beyond reason. A terrified woman with a gun. I used Sarah for negotiation once before, and she's good.'

'You won't put Sarah in the firing line?'

'She's a cop. A good cop. Sure, she's a medical specialist, but she's also done basic training in police work. This is her job.'

'Right,' Alistair managed, and Larry gave him a strange look.

'Look, I don't put my officers in the firing line without due cause,' he told him. 'But Sarah's a woman, and that might help. Besides…' Larry gave a rueful grin. 'It's more than my life is worth not to tell Sarah what's going on. The lady has a temper.'

Alistair had to agree with that. 'She has.'

Another strange look—but Larry didn't have time to waste on anything but imperatives. 'Let's move, then,' he snapped. 'I don't want anyone working alone. Max, do you want to help?'

'I sure do.'

'Then how about waking any locals who might be useful and organising teams? We're not trying to arrest this woman—I want no one going near her until I have Sarah on hand to help—but I want to find signs of where she might be.

Alistair, I want you to stay here. If the woman's stealing medical supplies then maybe she'll figure that she needs a doctor. I want you to be here if she comes back.'

'But…'

'Stay,' Larry snapped. 'But wake Sarah for me.'

'Sure.' He had no choice. Alistair left them and strode around to the doctor's quarters.

Sarah's bedroom door was wide open. She was gone.

Alistair was worried, but Larry wasn't. 'We can't wait.' The detective was annoyed, but not concerned. Sarah's nightgown was neatly folded and her bed made. Every sign said she'd gone somewhere of her own accord. 'What a day to decide for a morning walk.'

He checked his watch. 'We were supposed to be leaving at six,' he told Alistair. 'That's in less than an hour, but by then there'll be more sand obliterating tracks. We'll move without her.' He motioned to the radio on his belt. 'Contact me the minute she gets back and I'll organise to meet her. We leave now.'

Barry watched the searchers leave—a team of the police force's crack searchers with locals attached.

No one had come near him. No one wanted him. He was a cop with local knowledge and they didn't want him. The thought made him feel so angry he was almost numb with rage.

He could tell them where to look. He could.

Not one of them came near him. No one asked his advice. The knot of resentment and rage twisted his gut until he felt as if he was going to vomit. But as he settled—as he watched the last of them leave—the resentment turned to a fierce determination.

He could do this.

His gun was still in the safe at the back of the police station. His suspension wasn't official yet. Larry might have the clout to take him off the case—to tell him to take leave pending an inquiry—but he didn't have the authority to do more. So if he discovered whoever was out there north of the town he could make an arrest. It might have to be a citizen's arrest, but it'd still be an arrest.

They'd look pretty stupid when they came back from a day's hunting and he had them safely in the lock-up.

It might even help.

If he'd been taken off the case then he shouldn't wear uniform. He should wear plain clothes.

But the pain in his gut was still there. The fury. He was a cop. He was a bloody good cop. Why shouldn't he wear what he liked?

He liked his uniform.

And he liked his gun.

Determination building by the minute, he dressed and loaded his gun. He checked that no one was watching and made his way outside.

He turned north.

'Noa, we need to take Azron to hospital.'

There was no answer. The woman had her back to the cliff face. The gun was pointing straight at Sarah.

Sarah had done all she could. She'd set up a drip. Fluids were the most important thing. The child had lost far too much blood and his fluids were badly depleted. Even if his father was a doctor, there were limits to what he'd have been able to do.

The child should have had plasma and saline two days ago.

She didn't have plasma now. She only had the saline that had been with Alistair's kit.

And antibiotics. She had them running through the drip now—thankfully Alistair's bag was really well equipped—but the child's rampant infection needed stronger ones than she had available.

She'd checked the wound. It had been cleaned but it needed

debridement, and Sarah was fairly certain that slivers of metal were still embedded deep.

She wanted X-rays. More—she wanted an intensive care unit. He must be severely anaemic. His whole body seemed to be shutting down. His breathing was so weak. There was no oxygen. She had a mask, but no cylinder.

'Noa, please...'

'Just fix him.' The woman's voice was harsh.

'You need help yourself.'

'No.'

Sarah sat back and looked at her. Looked at her drained, exhausted eyes. Looked at the stained bandage around her wrist.

'Let me help you.'

'No one can help me.'

'I can help you,' Sarah said softly. 'I'm a doctor. I have nothing to do with the man who shot your husband. I have nothing to do with the immigration authorities. All I know is that you're in trouble.'

'No.'

'At least drink something.' Sarah made a movement to the stockpile of water and the woman's hand jerked. The gun followed Sarah.

This was hopeless. Dreadful.

'I'm getting you water. And then I'm going to treat your arm.'

'Look after my son.'

'I've done all I can for Azron. He's in the shade. He's being rehydrated. I've started antibiotics. But when your husband and your son are both well then they'll need you. You need to be well, Noa.'

'Stay...'

'I'm not going to stay,' Sarah said, keeping her voice soft and steady. Her eyes didn't leave Noa's face. 'I'm going to look at your arm. You can shoot me if you must, but that's a

really stupid thing to do. All I want is to help you. Point the
gun at me all you want. But I'm helping.'

In the house next to the general store Mariette saw the searchers and made her own decision. Donny had been vomiting
intermittently all night and it had gone on too long. She was
starting to worry. If the search team was out, then surely Dr
Benn would be awake?

She phoned, and three minutes later Alistair appeared.

'I'm glad of the work,' he told her as he gave Donny an
injection. The little boy was dehydrated, but the metoclopram-
ide worked fast. This tummy infection had been spreading
through the local schoolchildren and he wasn't too concerned.
'I'm not very good at staying behind waiting for news.'

'I imagine you'd all be worried,' Mariette told him as she
saw him out. 'I wish there was some way I could help. All
I've done so far is donate a sheet.'

'Donate a sheet?'

So she told him about the missing sheet, and as she did
Alistair's unease deepened. There was someone else near
town, then? Was someone hiding closer than the wreck?

Where was Sarah?

He didn't want to wait, he thought fiercely. He wanted her
back here *now*!

By the time he returned to the hospital it was six o'clock,
and his concern was growing by the minute. Sarah's bedroom
remained ordered and neat. No one had broken into the hospital. Flotsam would have barked. Nothing was out of place.

She must have gone out of her own free will.

She wouldn't have walked south. He sensed that. When
he'd left her, her emotions would have been in as great a
turmoil as his. How could she have slept?

She wouldn't. If he was Sarah…

She would have gone to the beach, he decided. She would
have walked into the rising sun, north-east, where the dawn
was a glowing fragile beauty.

He knew it. He knew it in his gut.

So was she out walking now? Still?

Surely not. She would have known that the searchers were leaving early and she'd said she'd go with them. She was here to do a job. No matter what turmoil her life had become, her job was still important to her. She cared about the people in the plane.

She wouldn't have forgotten.

He paced. The little hospital slept. No one needed him.

He should stay. He should stay and wait.

But more and more his gut was telling him something was wrong. Who had taken that sheet? Where were they?

He was going nuts.

'Claire…' He walked through to the nurses' station and found the charge nurse. 'Claire, I'm going out for a bit.'

'I thought you were supposed to stay within calling range.' Claire put her head on one side and surveyed him with interest. 'Are you heading towards the wreck, then?'

'No,' he said shortly. 'I'm going for a walk. Along the beach. North.'

'Taking Flotsam?'

'No.'

Claire frowned. 'Is that where you think Sarah might have gone?'

'It might be,' Alistair said shortly, and left before her bright interest could respond with questions he had no way of answering.

It took patience and courage to work with that gun quivering so close to her, but by the time Sarah had rebandaged Noa's arm and forced her to drink and to eat the woman had stopped her fearful trembling. Azron started to stir, just a little, and on instinct Sarah lifted the tiny boy and carried him to his mother. It was tricky with the bags of fluid, but she managed.

Noa watched without saying a word.

Sarah stood before her and held out the child. 'Hold him,' she said.

'I need to hold the gun.'

'I'll sit here,' Sarah said. 'You can hold the gun in your right hand—your uninjured hand—with Azron cradled on your knee. He needs your warmth. He needs you.'

Noa hesitated. The gun wavered. Sarah stood, holding the child, her eyes calm and steady.

The woman needed time, Sarah thought. She wouldn't pressure her more than she already had. She'd eaten a little and she'd drunk a full bottle of water. If she could settle with her child in her arms, maybe she could gradually learn to trust.

Maybe.

And there was time. She wouldn't rush. Azron's need was still urgent, but he was being rehydrated. There were antibiotics running into his system. Establishing trust with his mother was the only way forward.

'Hold him,' she said again, and Azron opened his eyes—just a fraction—and whimpered.

It was too much. Noa gave a tiny choking sob and held out her arms.

Sarah could have moved then. She could have grabbed the gun. But there was a risk it might have gone off—a risk she wasn't prepared to take.

Patience.

She lowered the child onto Noa's knee, then backed against the cliff and sat. She carefully stayed within range. She carefully stayed where the gun could easily point at her without Noa straining.

'What now?' she asked.

'We wait.' Noa was clutching Azron and Sarah saw that her need for contact was almost overwhelming. She had no clue how to go forward. But now wasn't the time to push her further.

'Okay. I'm happy with that. Let's wait a while until you

see your way forward,' she agreed. She sat and let the silence drag out.

Noa's eyes flickered to Sarah, to the face of her son, to the cleft in the rock face through which a threat might come…

Her eyes were exhausted.

'Tell me about yourself,' Sarah said gently. 'Tell me what happened to drive you from your country.'

'No.' Noa shook her head, fierce in denial. 'No.' Then she hesitated. 'You…you tell me. Tell me about you. Are you married?'

'No.'

'So you have no children?'

'No.'

'It's good to have children.' The woman clutched Azron a little tighter, and then seemed to make a determined effort to concentrate on Sarah.

'Why aren't you married? Has no man asked you?'

'One man did,' Sarah said softly. 'A long time ago. And at first I said yes. But then I turned him down.'

Noa's eyes caught hers. And held. Woman to woman.

This was the first trace of something away from her nightmare, Sarah thought. A tiny vestige of normality. One woman talking relationships with another.

'You turned him down?'

'Yes.'

'Why?'

'It's a long story.'

'Tell me,' Noa whispered. 'While we wait for my son to get well…you tell me.'

Which one?

There were so many caves around here. The sand had obliterated the barrow marks. It had to be easy walking distance, though. She couldn't have got far.

Barry moved from cleft to cleft, his gun at the ready, staying in shadows.

Where…?

'Bastards,' he whispered. 'They've ruined my career. Bastards…'

His finger tightened on the trigger.

Where?

Half a mile out of town Alistair found Barry. Or he saw him. He glimpsed him in the distance at first. Alistair walked on, but instinctively moved closer to the cliffs, staying out of sight.

What on earth was Barry doing here? He was in full uniform, climbing along the cliff face.

Gun raised.

Alistair melted backwards. Maybe he should call out. Should he? This was Barry, after all. He was a police officer.

But…he was a suspended police officer. Alistair had watched Barry's face yesterday as they'd carried Amal away and he'd worried. Barry had looked at the wounded man and the expression on his face had been almost one of satisfaction. That look had disturbed him, and he'd passed on his concern to Larry. The man needed full psychological assessment.

He needed help.

Larry should have taken his gun away from him, Alistair thought. But to take his firearm… Well, it obviously hadn't occurred to Larry. Barry wasn't a criminal. He'd been far too over-zealous, and there was no way he could stay in the force after yesterday, but to strip him of uniform and gun straight away probably wasn't in Larry's jurisdiction.

And maybe it hadn't seemed necessary.

But now… Now Alistair made a choice. He wouldn't call out. The way Barry was moving scared him, he decided. The way he held the gun.

What on earth was he doing?

Alistair watched.

The big policeman seemed to be searching the cliff face, moving swiftly over the shale towards a cleft just above him.

Alistair frowned, growing more uneasy by the minute. What did Barry know that they didn't?

Where was Sarah?

Making a swift decision, he pulled back, out of sight behind a rock face. Lifting his cellphone, he dialled Larry. Okay, Larry was involved in an urgent police search, south of town, but Alistair didn't like what was happening here one bit. There were things that didn't fit.

What was Barry doing out here? The man was suspended. He had no business wearing his uniform. He had no business holding a gun.

Where was Sarah?

'Larry?' he said into the phone, keeping his voice low. 'Larry, I think I need help. I'll tell you what's happening. Listen…'

Behind the cliff face, things were easier.

The last half-hour had been spent establishing trust. Azron seemed to have stabilised. His breathing was easier, his pulse was strengthening and he seemed naturally asleep in his mother's arms. Sarah felt that her decision not to push things had been justified.

And Noa?

She'd listened as Sarah had told her story. It was a pathetic tale, Sarah decided—a story of loving one twin too much and one too little—but it had served its purpose. Noa's body seemed to have relaxed, some of the awful tension easing. At the end her questions had been thoughtful and sympathetic, and Sarah had thought, Who was treating who?

But it was good. It had turned the tables just a little, giving Noa back a trace of her dignity. It was a tiny taste of normality in a world that was no longer normal.

And then there was the sound of footsteps. Shale slipping down the cliff face. Someone approaching.

Sarah was sitting by the cleft. She couldn't see.

But Noa…Noa could see. Noa could hear. The fear which

had blessedly eased over the last few minutes came flooding back. Her gun jerked upward, waving from Sarah to the cleft and back.

'Move. Sideways.'

'Noa, I don't know who this is, but it'll be a friend.' Sarah's voice was urgent. 'Please. Let me see who it is. Let me stop them.'

'Move.' Noa was on her feet, clutching her son hard against her, her hand somehow still controlling the gun. She glanced behind her to the north face, where the shale of the cliff face rose at an almost forty-five-degree angle. 'Move away from the entrance.'

Sarah moved. About a foot. Her eyes didn't leave Noa's gun.

'Whoever it is, stay where you are!' Sarah called out. 'We're fine. Noa's fine. Don't come closer.'

That'd stop Larry, she thought. He'd get her urgency. He'd stop.

The footsteps paused.

Then... 'Whoever's in there, I have you covered. Get out now. Come out now with your hands up.'

Barry.

It was Barry. His voice was deep and low and unmistakable.

Sarah's gaze flew back to Noa and she saw that Noa knew exactly who was out there. The man who had shot her husband.

She was holding her injured son.

She was trapped.

'No,' Noa whispered. She cast an anguished look at Sarah—as if for just a moment she'd learned to trust and that trust had been dreadfully betrayed—and then she turned to the cliff.

'You can't climb—' Sarah took a step towards her but the gun whirled back.

'Don't stop me. We must.' The woman hauled the ends of

her gown around her son and tied them hard, hauling the little boy into her body with a skill that must have been learned from generations of women who suffered with children in terror-torn countries. And then she took her first steps up the rock face.

The shale slipped.

Noa held. Her feet, in flimsy rope sandals, gripped the shale. She moved upward.

How could she hold on? *How?*

'Noa, no!'

'Stop or I'll shoot!'

Barry was standing in the cleft in full uniform, his two hands holding his gun. Whether he meant the threat or not, he was pointing it straight at Noa.

Noa turned back to face him. Wavering. It was impossible for her to climb. Impossible.

So she did the only thing left to her. Leaning back against the shale, somehow balancing, she raised her gun towards Barry.

'No!'

Sarah screamed. One yell that split the morning. She dived straight across, launching herself at Barry's gun hand. He whirled.

She grabbed and pulled. 'No!'

A searing, white-hot pain.

'No…!'

From where he stood behind a rock face Alistair heard Sarah call out.

'Whoever it is, stay where you are! We're fine. Noa's fine. Don't come closer.'

Alistair dropped the phone and started forward. He saw Barry move into the cleft.

In the background he heard Larry's voice, urgent over the phone, but he ignored it.

'*Whoever's in there, I have you covered. Get out now. Come out now with your hands up.*'

Dear God…

All he could see was Barry's back. Then he was running, covering the yards to the foot of the cliff. Starting to climb.

'*Stop or I'll shoot!*'

'*No!*'

Sarah! He was flying. He hadn't known his body could move so fast. But not fast enough. Not—

'*No…!*'

Sarah's scream froze his heart. And then the crack of a pistol shot.

No!

He launched himself forward in a rugby tackle that he hadn't known he remembered.

He hit Barry square on and they flew forward together in the dust. Barry's hand still gripped the gun, but Alistair had him, tackling him to the ground with a strength born of terror. As they smashed into the ground his fingers found what they so desperately sought. They found the gun. Wrenched. Barry turned. Alistair's knee came up in an age-old method of self-defence that was pure instinct.

Barry grunted in agony and the pistol flew.

At the cliff face, a woman with a child-shaped bundle roped to her body was sliding down the shale. Alistair had no time to see. Barry was hauling back his fist but Alistair was before him, smashing, working with a strength he'd never known he had. Never dreamed he could use. He hit. Hit again.

And Barry slumped.

Enough. The threat momentarily allayed, Alistair whirled to find the woman standing staring down at him. With a pistol in each hand.

Beside her was Sarah. Sarah… There was a crease of crimson on her forehead. She lay limp and lifeless in the sand.

'Sarah…' He moved, but the woman stopped him. She

stepped between Alistair and Sarah and the pistols pointed straight at his heart.

'Wh…who are you?' she whispered.

'Alistair.' It was a stupid thing to say. A really stupid thing to say. But he'd gone past thinking. All he could see was Sarah. All he could think of was Sarah.

'You're Sarah's Alistair?' Noa whispered, and Alistair nodded. How on earth she'd known he couldn't tell, but he was past disputing such a basic part of his being.

Sarah's Alastair…

'Yes. Yes, I am.'

The woman looked at him for a long, long moment. And then her body seemed to slump. She turned to where Barry was hauling himself together, gathering himself to lash out again.

The guns moved away from Alistair and pointed straight at Barry.

'Stay where you are!' she spat. 'Stay.' Her glance moved to Sarah. 'Alistair,' she whispered, as if it was a mantra. 'Sarah's Alistair. Please. Save Sarah. Help Sarah. We need… help.'

CHAPTER ELEVEN

THE second helicopter was ready to leave at dusk. It took away Larry's élite police squad, and also Barry—in handcuffs, being taken to Brisbane to face criminal charges.

Larry was the last on the chopper. He'd apologised so many times Alistair had been forced to reassure him.

'It's not your fault.'

'No, but Barry's a cop, and when one of our own goes bad…well, we all feel it.'

'But you fixed it.' Alistair gave a rueful smile as they stood beside the waiting helicopter. 'I never knew the results of a telephone call could be so amazing. How long did it take you to reach us?'

'God knows. I heard that shot down the phoneline and I forget how fast I moved,' Larry told him. 'I came closer than I ever want to come again to having a heart attack.'

'I was having one of my own,' Alistair admitted. He hesitated. 'You'll see that Noa and Azron are safe?'

'They're already in Cairns,' Larry told him. The first evacuation helicopter had left some hours before, with Noa and Azron and a full medical team aboard. 'I had a radio message just now. Word is that the little one's stable. The doctors think he'll make it. Thanks to you.'

'Thanks to Sarah.'

'Mmm.' They'd stared out into the dusk. It had taken time to organise the second helicopter flight, giving them time to think things through.

'What do you think will happen?' Alistair asked, and Larry gave a rueful smile.

'To who? To Barry? I suspect he'll end up in a psychiatric institution. He seems to have lost all logic. To the people behind this racket? The police in Sydney have moved to arrest the ringleader. The smuggling ring is smashed. Howard might end up in jail, but he's small fry. He might get off with a suspended sentence. The guy behind it, though, will be put away for a very long time. Robbing people who are terrified for their lives… Jail's too good for him. And as for Noa and Amal and Azron—their story will be checked, but if it holds water, and I have no reason to suspect it won't, then they'll be granted refugee status and cared for. The word from Cairns is that Amal is going to pull through. They've been very lucky.'

'Or very unlucky. Depending how you look at it.'

'As you say.' The helicopter was loaded, they were waiting for Larry, and Larry turned to grip Alistair's hand. 'Thanks, mate. Invite me to your wedding, will you?'

Alistair paused. 'What?'

'Are you arguing?'

And Alistair grinned. 'No,' he said at last. 'No, I'm not.'

The ward was in darkness.

Sarah had come round almost at once, surfacing to chaos. Noa weeping. Barry shouting obscenities. Alistair swearing, over and over again, but his fingers so tender as they probed the pain across her forehead. Larry and his men bursting through the cleft, barking instructions.

Being held by Alistair…

And then Alistair having to leave her. The jolting had made Azron's leg bleed. He had to focus on the little boy. But he was still there, supervising as one of the men held a pressure pack above the crease line made by the bullet across her forehead, making sure she wasn't jolted as she was carried into a waiting truck, refusing to even consider her protest that she was okay, she could walk…

He'd been with her to show her the results of X-rays—X-rays that showed she'd been concussed by the force of the bullet but that it had grazed her and done no substantial injury.

He'd held her briefly—so briefly.

He'd been needed. So needed.

Azron had needed him and so had Noa, and then when they had left there was Barry, who'd needed sedating, and Howard, who had still been yelling in pain and anxiety, and a kid who'd had the temerity to come in with an earache in the middle of the drama.

The nurses, following instructions, had tucked her into the ward and given her something that made her sleepy, had darkened the room and checked her every now and then...

Had let her sleep.

She had. And now it was dark, and she opened her eyes and Alistair was standing in the doorway. Just looking. Not moving.

'Alistair...'

It was a whisper, but it was enough.

He covered the distance between door and bed in an instant and she was gathered in his arms. She was being held. Cradled. Held against his chest, her breasts moulding to him, feeling the beat of his heart against hers.

She was where she most wanted to be.

Home.

'Alistair...'

'I thought I'd lost you,' he murmured, his face in her hair. 'Sarah, I thought you'd gone. I heard you scream and I thought... I thought...'

'Hush.'

He shook his head, holding her slightly away from him so he could see her face in the dim light.

'We've been fools,' he told her. 'We've wasted time.'

'No...'

'Sarah, shut up and listen,' he said, but there was such a wealth of loving behind his words that she could hardly take offence. She could hardly take it in. 'I love you,' he told her. 'I've loved you for six long years and more, and I love you still. And if you let me… If you let me then I intend to love you for the rest of your life.'

'But—'

'Hush.' It was his turn to silence her. He laid her back on the pillows and put a finger against her lips. 'I think it's time we explained. It's time we talked. You see, I fell in love with you the first time I saw you. Doing that crazy crab walk at the children's hospital. But of course you were Grant's girl-friend. I was going out with someone else, and I told myself I was a fool. I couldn't want what Grant had.'

'But—'

'But then you came to the farm for Christmas,' he contin-ued. 'Do you know how close I came to breaking? You were so near. And Grant kept leaving and you were there, laughing, loving, making my parents love you, making me love you…'

'You had a girlfriend.'

'No. I broke up with Rachel before that week was out. I knew what I felt for you was impossible, but I also knew it was impossible to keep up any relationship with anyone else while I felt like I did. But you were still going out with Grant, and then he rang and said you'd agreed to marry him.'

'I was so in love with your family,' she whispered. 'I thought… I had it all mixed up. But it was a mistake.'

'Noa told me.' He closed his eyes and took her hands in his. 'It took a terrified refugee with all the world to lose to make me see the truth. We talked while we were waiting for the plane to come. Azron was asleep and I was treating her wrist. I asked her why she'd described me as ''Sarah's Alistair'' and she told me the story you'd told her. She told me that you loved me. That you'd realised you were marrying Grant not for him but for his family—for me! That you loved Grant only because he was so like me. But he wasn't the same. And as soon as you realised you broke off your en-gagement. Is that true, Sarah?'

Sarah gazed up at him, stunned. Noa had told him this? In

the face of her terror Noa had taken this in and felt it important enough to tell Alistair? 'Yes, but...'

'And you weren't engaged to Grant when the car crashed?'

'No.'

'He hadn't told us.'

'He didn't want me to break it off. He was still trying to make me change my mind.'

'And you wouldn't?'

'I loved you,' she said softly. 'I fell so hard... Over Christmas. Every time you smiled... And the only way I could get near that smile was to marry Grant. But of course it wasn't enough. It wasn't nearly enough.'

'And then Grant was killed.' Alistair was holding her so tight he was hurting—but not hurting. How could he hurt her? 'If you knew how I felt... I loved you, and yet everything was screaming at me that it was crazy. As far as I knew you were still engaged to my twin. And he was dead. You were driving when you shouldn't have been. There was grief...so much grief for my twin. And my parents were bereft, and then ill. I couldn't cope with the way I felt about you. I couldn't begin to think about you...like that. And all along...'

'Alistair...'

'Enough.' He was still holding her, but his grip had slackened a little. He put a hand up and traced the bandage across her forehead. 'I've come so close this day. So close to losing the most precious thing in the world. I'll not let that happen again. Do you hear?'

'Not?' There was a searing joy exploding around her heart. Joy coursing through her veins, taking over her world. Joy...

How could this thing suddenly be so right? How could so much grief suddenly be made right? And yet it was. Here was her man. Her partner. Her life's meet.

Alistair...

She didn't speak. She didn't have to. She was gazing at him and all the joy in her heart was right there in her eyes.

She was gathered into his arms and she was melting into

him. His lips were claiming hers, their hearts were merging, heartbeats beating with a single rhythm.

Pain becoming joy.

Two becoming one.

All they needed was a wedding…

CHAPTER TWELVE

DAWN.

Dawn at Dolphin Cove. It was a strange time for a wedding, but here in the north where the searing heat took over in the middle of the day no one was complaining. No one was complaining at all.

Every man and his dog was here.

Larry was here, with so many police squad members—friends Sarah had hardly known she had. Max was best man. Claire was bridesmaid, beaming with proprietary joy.

Every person in the district seemed to be on the beach this morning.

And every dog.

Flotsam was here—of course. The little dog was busier than ever these days, with a new pup demanding his full attention. The black and white ball of cocker spaniel fluff was the town's get-well gift to Azron. Appropriately or not, the town had voted his name as Jetsam.

They wore wonderful red ribbons—and why not? It was such an occasion. The fishermen had fashioned a guard of honour, using fishing nets as a gorgeous canopy instead of upraised swords. They'd provided the basis for the wedding breakfast laid on in marquees on the beach. Seafood to die for. Crays, bugs, oysters, prawns. And cakes and pastries that the district women had been planning for months. Every local was doing his utmost to see that this wedding was one that would last.

Well, why wouldn't they? In Alistair they had a doctor in a million, and this new lady doctor met with general approval.

For Sarah had taken her third career step without a backward glance. First a paediatrician. Second a forensic pathologist. And now here she was, a country doctor with a little police work on the side, helping out the brand-new sergeant of police—one of Larry's men, who'd fallen in love with the place and asked to stay.

It fitted beautifully. Sarah still had time to continue with the police work she'd grown to enjoy. And Dolphin Cove, once medically understaffed, now threatened to be a medical mecca for the north. Because there was another doctor here, too.

Amal was here, with his wife and his son. All fully recovered. Gloriously recovered. The Dolphin Cove community had offered to sponsor the little family, and it seemed everyone in town had wanted to take a hand in providing a safe and comfortable home for these people whose introduction to this country had been so harsh.

It was working out so well. Alistair was mentoring Amal as he did the retraining necessary to work as a doctor in this strange new country. Maybe when he qualified he would move to a bigger place, but for now Azron was at kindergarten here, and loving it, Noa had been taken under the wing of the local women, and the little family was blooming.

Azron was pageboy, beaming with pride at his responsibilities, and his parents beamed with joy at this, their first wedding in this wonderful new home. Sarah had asked Noa to be her matron of honour, but Noa had blushed and declined. She'd laid her hand on her tummy and smiled and smiled.

'It is very early. Very early. I feel…sometimes a little sick. I would prefer not to spoil your day.'

How could she spoil it? There was so much happiness here for all of them. But Sarah wouldn't push her. This little family who'd been through so much had found a home here in the most unexpected of places.

It seemed they were here to stay.

And Sarah? And Alistair?

They were here to stay, too. Of course they were.

They stood on the beach with their faces turned towards the rising sun, and they made their vows in voices that told every watching person that there was no mistaking their sincerity. Their love. Their joy.

No one who saw them could doubt that this man and this woman were meant for each other.

From this day forth.

For ever.

MILLS & BOON®

Live the emotion

_Medical
romance™

A DOCTOR'S CHRISTMAS FAMILY
by Meredith Webber

Dr Esther Shaw, called home to Australia to battle a serious medical emergency, meets the last person she expects: Dr Bill Jackson – her ex-husband! Bill is managing the potentially deadly epidemic, taking care of an adorable baby – and trying to persuade his beautiful ex-wife to fall in love with him again…

THE MIDWIFE'S NEW YEAR WISH *by Jennifer Taylor*

(Dalverston)

It's Christmas time at Dalverston General, and midwife Katie Denning is frantically trying to find a stand-in Santa for the carol concert. Gorgeous stranger Nick Lawson steps in at the last minute, but it isn't until after he's claimed his fee – an earth-shattering kiss! – that she discovers he's the new Obs & Gynae registrar!

A DOCTOR TO COME HOME TO *by Gill Sanderson*

After a passionate fling on the sun-drenched island of Majorca, district nurse Amy Harrison never expected to see Dr Adam Ross again. Her previous marriage had made her afraid of relationships and she was scared of being hurt. But when Adam unexpectedly joined her Derbyshire practice Amy knew she had to face up to her past and take a chance on the future.

Don't miss out…

On sale 3rd December 2004

WE VALUE YOUR OPINION!

YOUR CHANCE TO WIN A ONE YEAR SUPPLY OF YOUR FAVOURITE BOOKS.

If you are a regular UK reader of Mills & Boon® Medical Romance™ and have always wanted to share your thoughts on the books you read—here's your chance:

Join the Reader Panel today!

This is your opportunity to let us know exactly what you think of the books you love.

And there's another great reason to join:

Each month, all members of the Reader Panel have a chance of winning four of their favourite Mills & Boon romance books EVERY month for a whole year!

If you would like to be considered for the Reader Panel, please complete and return the following application. Unfortunately, as we have limited spaces, we cannot guarantee that everyone will be selected.

Name: _____

Address: _____

_____ Post Code: _____

Home Telephone: _____ Email Address: _____

Where do you normally get your Mills & Boon Medical Romance books (please tick one of the following)?

Shops ☐   Library/Borrowed ☐

Reader Service™ ☐ If so, please give us your subscription no. _____

Please indicate which age group you are in:

16 – 24 ☐   25 – 34 ☐

35 – 49 ☐   50 – 64 ☐   65 + ☐

If you would like to apply by telephone, please call our friendly Customer Relations line on **020 8288 2886**, or get in touch by email to readerpanel@hmb.co.uk

Don't delay, apply to join the Reader Panel today and help ensure the range and quality of the books you enjoy.

Send your application to:

The Reader Service, Reader Panel Questionnaire, FREEPOST NAT1098, Richmond, TW9 1BR

If you do not wish to receive any additional marketing material from us, please contact the Data Manager at the address above.

FREE

4 BOOKS AND A SURPRISE GIFT!

We would like to take this opportunity to thank you for reading this
Mills & Boon® book by offering you the chance to take FOUR more
specially selected titles from the Medical Romance™ series absolutely
FREE! We're also making this offer to introduce you to the benefits of
the Reader Service™—

- ★ **FREE home delivery**
- ★ **FREE gifts and competitions**
- ★ **FREE monthly Newsletter**
- ★ **Books available before they're in the shops**
- ★ **Exclusive Reader Service offers**

Accepting these FREE books and gift places you under no obligation
to buy; you may cancel at any time, even after receiving your free
shipment. Simply complete your details below and return the entire
page to the address below. You don't even need a stamp!

YES! Please send me 4 free Medical Romance books and a surprise
gift. I understand that unless you hear from me, I will receive 6
superb new titles every month for just £2.69 each, postage and packing
free. I am under no obligation to purchase any books and may cancel
my subscription at any time. The free books and gift will be mine to
keep in any case.

M4ZEE

Ms/Mrs/Miss/Mr...Initials ....

BLOCK CAPITALS PLEASE

Surname ....

Address ....

....

....Postcode ....

Send this whole page to:
The Reader Service, FREEPOST CN81, Croydon, CR9 3WZ